J. Meredith Thomas

The Professor and His Daughters

A novel. Part 3

J. Meredith Thomas

The Professor and His Daughters
A novel. Part 3

ISBN/EAN: 9783337045838

Printed in Europe, USA, Canada, Australia, Japan

Cover: Foto ©Andreas Hilbeck / pixelio.de

More available books at **www.hansebooks.com**

THE
PROFESSOR AND HIS DAUGHTERS.

A Novel.

BY

J. MEREDITH THOMAS.

'Who shall set a limit to the direful consequences that may follow upon one false step! No life is absolutely by itself; it forms the centre of others that radiate from it like the spokes of a wheel, and that have to bear—so pitiless is Fate—their share of the penalties engendered by its weaknesses and follies. Here is food for thought.'—*From the German.*

IN THREE VOLUMES.

VOL. III.

London :

REMINGTON AND CO.,

134, NEW BOND STREET, W.

1883.

THE
PROFESSOR AND HIS DAUGHTERS.

BOOK V.—*Continued.*

CHAPTER III.

DEADMEN'S COURT, in spite of its dismal name, is a locality that improves upon acquaintance. If society in a measure avoids it, it is for that very reason rendered a pleasant retreat where stiff social rules may be quite disregarded. While Belgrave Square turns its nose in disgust from the man who saunters along without observing the formality of wearing a shirt, Deadmen's Court doesn't care a rap even though the passing stranger exhibit himself in the somewhat scanty but inexpensive dress of Mother Nature. It is perfectly free-and-easy, and has for its motto, 'Let everyone do as he likes.' Besides, it possesses those excellent qualities of being peaceful and quiet which many a fashionable West End square lacks, and the houses, though sombre and uninviting without, may be made very tolerable within.

Such were Charles's thoughts after he had passed a few weeks in his new residence; and, when he had done several things which would have involved a notice to quit in the ordinary 'respectable lodgings,' he voted it not such a bad place after all.

He met with no interference, not even from Dick. Indeed, he and his friend—or, as Charles in his own mind termed him, his servant—met only occasionally, and then but few words passed between them. This was not from any fault on Dick's part, but from the fact that Charles, having raised some money on certain useless articles purchased by him at considerable expense during his prosperity, had gone, to use his own words, 'on the spree,' and spent most of his time away from the court.

The image of the girl whom he had ruined had long since passed from Charles's memory, and the great scheme seemed in danger of sharing the same fate, for Dick carefully refrained from making any reference to it. Whatever projects the latter had in his mind, in which he needed Charles's assistance, were never mentioned by him; he waited patiently, knowing well that, until his purse had been first exhausted, Charles would submit to no control. When they met of a morning, Dick would quietly ask his friend :

' What are your intentions to-day, sir ?'

Charles would reply that he had an engagement here or there, and would be absent all day, whereupon Dick would nod his head slowly, and then cast his eyes upon the ceiling for a few moments as though engaged in a mental calculation.

Charles, indeed, was ' going it ' in the most thorough fashion, and was daily making inroads upon a constitution naturally delicate. But what did that matter ? Youth acts; old age thinks. All the worse for old age—when it comes. Possibly, there is no more wretched fate than that of the middle-aged man whose early debauchery has earned him a valetudinarian's crown—who passes his hours in looking back regretfully on the splendid constitution so foolishly squandered. Such retrospects are outraged nature's punishment.

Though Dick had led Charles to believe that Deadmen's Court was frequently honoured by visits from his numerous friends, yet, as time went on, Charles felt very much inclined to doubt the statement. The fact was that, with one exception, the friends had shown a most deplorable want of politeness; they seemed to have completely forgotten Dick's existence. They studiously refrained from showing themselves in Deadmen's Court.

Dick felt hurt at such shabby conduct, and frequently inveighed against his friends in warm terms, while Charles stood by with an insolent sneer on his lips which, if translated into words, would have meant, ' You are an excellent liar, but you cannot hoodwink me !'

The exception among this uncourteous band was a young man of about Charles's own age, with a fine, fresh countenance, ornamented on the upper lip with a soft, white down. He had a look of extreme simplicity, but his manners and conversation showed a refinement which Charles had hardly expected to meet with in a friend of Dick's. He came occasionally to the house, and took some commands from Dick, of what nature Charles did not trouble to inquire. He seldom spoke to Charles, and then only with much reserve; but he made up for the fewness of his words by the deferential tone in which he uttered them. His name was Alfred Pillbury.

Charles was rather amused by Mr. Pillbury's innocent appearance, and mentioned the fact to Dick in one of their occasional conversations.

'He looks about the biggest muff in creation,' he said. 'What the deuce can you make of such a fellow ?'

Dick smiled in his usual bland manner.

'He is very useful to me,' he answered. 'Perhaps his very appearance adds to his worth. He does look green, I admit, but for that reason people would never have any fear of being gulled by him. They don't look behind him; if they did, they'd see the string with which I work him. Ha ! ha !'

'A pigeon, eh ? Ha ! ha ! By Jove, Dick, I can't help admitting you've got a head on you. And the poor fool never suspects it ?'

'Oh, no. Don't tell him, sir, or you'll spoil the game. Ha ! ha ! His face is his fortune.'

'What does he do for you ?'

'Oh, various things—sporting transactions, et cætera. He was in want of a berth when I met him, sir, in consequence of some one or other having bolted with the money his father had left him. He helps me, and I help him. I don't pay him a great deal, but it's enough to keep body and soul in him, and that's something.'

' Where does he live ?'

' With his mother—a widow—Kennington way.'

' Well, if you lose him, you won't get such another in a hurry.'

' I hope I shan't lose him. If I do, sir,' added Dick, looking at Charles with a confident smile, ' I think I know where to lay my hands on one who could take his place.'

' You mightn't find his terms so easy.'

' Oh, I shouldn't fear on that score. I should take care to bind him to me by stronger ties than money ones.'

This conversation was followed in a very short time by another, in which, by the irony of fortune, Charles was obliged to play the unusual part of suppliant towards the companion whom, in his inmost mind, he despised in proportion as he received services at his hand.

He had spent nearly the whole of the money he had raised, and was in an awkward position. He had been compelled to refuse Miss Topsie Mandeville some small article of jewellery for which that estimable young lady had conceived a violent craving. Miss Mandeville was not accustomed to be met with a refusal when she had set her mind on anything, and, with a mighty show of spirit, she informed Charles that if his means did not enable him to bestow upon her a trumpery little article like the one in question, she begged to decline the honour of his further acquaintance. Charles flared up, and accused Miss Mandeville of being a mercenary young woman; and Miss Mandeville, in whose hands the English language could be made as expressive for offensive purposes as the most liquid of the tongues of the fiery South, made him an effective rejoinder. A very pretty quarrel followed, which ended—as all quarrels should—in a reconciliation, and a promise on Charles's part that the impertinent little piece of jewellery which had been the cause of their dispute should be in Miss Mandeville's possession within a very few days.

To redeem this promise, he hurried off to Deadmen's Court, thinking that Dick's ingenuity would discover some method of once more refilling his pockets.

His visit was apparently scarcely well-timed, for
Dick looked up with an expression of annoyance as
his visitor entered, and gave vent to a smothered
remark which could by no means have been twisted
into a friendly greeting. But he quickly composed
his features, and even allowed one of his blandest
smiles to play on his face. Charles had evidently
disturbed him in some important operation, for he
was seated close to the window, and his desk was
littered with papers. For the purposes of his work,
he had fixed a reflector to the one clean pane of
glass in the window at such an angle as to throw all
the available light full upon the blotting-pad immediately before him. Upon the blotting-pad was
what appeared to be an ordinary cheque. What
struck Charles's attention most was a small tin box
that stood by Dick's right hand, containing, among
other things, some small bottles, some fine brushes,
some coloured crayons, and some tracing paper.

'What mysterious business are you about?' he
asked.

'There is nothing very mysterious about it, sir,'
answered Dick composedly. 'I happen to have a
talent for drawing, which I am cultivating in case
of mishaps. It's a real pleasure to me, and, who

knows, may one day get me a meal when I'm in need of one. Look here, sir—not so very bad, is it?'

He held up a cleverly executed little etching, which he took from the tin box. Charles was no judge of art in any shape, but he seized the opportunity held out to him of indulging his vanity.

'Not badly done,' he said, in an affected, critical tone, as he examined it. 'Of course, one can see it's done by a beginner, but it's clever in a way. I wasn't aware that your talents ran in that direction.'

'One doesn't care to brag about these things,' said Dick modestly, as he leisurely gathered up the materials he had been using in his work, and placed them in the box.

The cheque had found its way quietly into his pocket while Charles was engaged in his critical examination of the etching. When he had locked the box, Dick turned to Charles with an inquiring glance.

'What is there that I can do for you, sir?' he asked.

Charles laughed lightly, and twisted in his chair;

he scarcely felt at his ease. He was about to beg a favour of a man whom he despised, and he fancied he detected in Dick's face a smile of triumph at his coming humiliation. He, however, nerved himself to the occasion, and put forward his request in his usual authoritative manner.

'I'm devilishly hard up,' he said, twisting the end of a youthful moustache, 'and I want money.'

Dick laughed playfully.

'That's the case with all of us, sir.'

'So it may be ; but still I can't do without it, and must have it. Do you see ?'

'I can quite understand the necessity, sir, for you've been pretty lavish lately——'

'Oh, hang all that ! Look here, you must get me some money.'

Dick put on an aggrieved expression.

'I am sorry, sir, if you take it offensive in me to speak of your lavishness. I only do it for the best. If I had any money, you should have it. But I have none.'

Charles bit his lips with vexation, and felt in-clined to give his friend a bit of his mind ; but, re-flecting on his promise to Miss Mandeville, he wisely checked his ill-temper, and in an humbler tone said :

'I don't object to your speaking to me about my lavishness, as you call it; but I can't help myself. I always was free with my money, and always shall be; so, you see, what can't be cured must be endured. I shouldn't ask for this money now if I didn't want it most particularly, and I am sure if you try you can get it for me.'

Dick shook his head.

'I'm afraid, sir, just now it's impossible. If you could wait for a month or two——'

'It would be no good at all. I must have it at once. In fact, I have promised some one—well, it's a lady—to buy her something, and I can't do it without money.'

Still Dick shook his head.

'I wish I could help you, sir, with all my heart, but I assure you——'

'Come, come, old fellow,' said Charles, rising from his chair, and laying his hand familiarly on Dick's shoulder, 'you mustn't refuse me. Only get it for me, and you shall lecture me as much as you please. I'll do anything you like to ask of me, or at least I'll try to; it's all the same.'

He paused, but Dick still bent his eyes moodily on the ground.

'Come, say, Dick, that you'll get this money for me. A hundred will do. Now, be a good fellow, and say "Yes." On my word, I'll make any return you like to ask for.'

Dick rose suddenly as if a bright idea had struck him.

'I think I may be able to manage it, sir; at least, I'll do my best. Come here the day after to-morrow, and, if my idea is worth anything, I don't think you will be disappointed.'

Charles thanked him with seeming cordiality, but as he passed out of the court he ground his teeth together and clenched his fists.

'Curse the fellow!' he muttered. 'He makes me put myself under obligations to him; but I'll be even with him some day. I'll let him know that there is some difference between a gentleman and a low blackguard like him!'

But, notwithstanding this bitter feeling, he attended punctually upon Dick at the time appointed, and had the satisfaction of finding that his friend's idea had met with the anticipated success.

CHAPTER IV.

IT is difficult to imagine any situation more full of bitterness than that of a young girl who, far away from home and friends, passes through the agonies of childbirth. The feeling of utter desolation, the imminence of deadly peril, the absence of the well-known voices—above all, the absence of him who at such a moment should be nigh to soothe her with his loving caresses—all go to make the situation terrible to contemplate.

This was our poor Omega's situation; yet, thanks to the kindness of her two fellow-lodgers, she passed through it safely, and woke from unconsciousness to find a little copy of herself nestling by her side.

From this moment she forgot her cares and trials. The past was to her a hideous dream to be banished from memory; the future, a grim reality, with one hopeful stream of light to illumine its darkness—her baby. She was a mother, and her heart beat with a strange vigour. Thus maternity, while giving her a new mouth to feed, gave her new strength to face the world.

The baby grew, and the mother's happiness grew with it; for there was still money in the purse. It had no formal christening, but the mother called it —after an old Welsh name—Angharad, which means, 'my darling.'

She played with it all day, and caressed it all night. It was her plaything and her lovething; more, it was her life.

One evening, when she and Sal were sitting together, watching the infant as it lay asleep in bed, Omega said :

'Isn't she lovely, Sal ? Oh, how I love her !'

Sal looked grave.

' My dear,' she said, ' she's a sweet little darling ; but 'ow are you goin' to keep her ?'

Omega laughed.

' What ! Do you fear for baby and me ? Oh, we shall never starve now that I have her.'

' You should have gone home.'

' Home ! I have done with home for ever. They never answered my letter; they have hard hearts. They have given me up; they have forgotten me.

Well, baby and I will forget them; we are quite enough for each other.'

' Write home again.'

'I?   Never!   I was foolish then, for I was alone; now I have my child to fill my mind.'

Sal said no more. It was not her business to think of the baby's future. She had done a friendly duty in bringing the subject before Omega, and, if the latter paid no attention, it was not her fault.

At this juncture Mary Ann came in, rigged out in her best.

' Ain't you a-comin' out, Sal ?' she asked.

' Don't be in such a bloomin' hurry, Mary Ann,' said Sal; 'this young lady and me is a-talking together—confidential.'

She winked at Omega for her to take notice how easily she could get Mary Ann's monkey up.

' Confidential, is it ?' cried Mary Ann, with a crimson cheek. ' She might choose somebody better than you if she 'ad to go to the workus for 'er. A mighty fine person you are, with a face like a pewter pot.'

' No hinsults, please, Mary Ann,' said Sal, haughtily. ' I know as you don't know any better, for you ain't 'ad no edication, but I won't bear bein' hinsulted from you.'

'Who are you, I should like to know?' exclaimed Mary Ann, in a fury. 'What was your mother? A charwoman! What was your father? A bloomin' old coster!'

Sal was significantly rolling up her sleeves, when Omega interposed.

'Please be quiet,' she said; 'you'll wake baby. Mary Ann, do please get a shilling'sworth of gin, and help Sal and me to drink it.'

'Anythin' to please you, I'm sure, my dear.'

Mary Ann left the room at once, and Sal, after remarking that her friend was a 'hignerant young woman,' quickly calmed down. Soon the two were toasting each other as if no shadow of a quarrel had ever come between their friendship, while Omega was laughing at their quaint phrases, and not neglecting her own share of the fiery liquor.

The two children, Bill and Nan, were constantly with Omega. They were both much interested in the baby, though Bill feigned a lordly contempt for 'the kid,' as he called it. While Nan would be sitting with it upon her knee, and, with the instinct of womanhood, would be trying to hush it to sleep,

Bill would stand by with his hands in his ragged pockets, and would utter profound remarks called up by the occasion.

'Blowed if the little cuss can see straight,' he said, one day, as the baby rested calmly on Nan's knee, with its eyes wandering vaguely round the room. 'I say, look at 'er—jes' look at 'er.'

'Baby will soon be able to see as well as you, Bill,' said Omega. 'Now I'm going to wash her face.'

'Blowed if I'd stand that!' exclaimed Bill. 'She 'ain't got 'alf a spirit. Ah! I thought she'd 'oller—go it, little 'un. Tune up! Ha! ha! By God she can 'owl!'

Omega paused in her work. The easy manner in which this immature lad took the name of his Maker in vain startled her, though she had long since ceased to remark the same peculiarity in his seniors.

'You are too young to swear, Bill,' she said, gently.

Bill looked up in astonishment.

'Who's swearin'?' he asked. 'Not me!'

He was right. There was no irreverence in what he had said; it was merely an ordinary phrase of the gutter language he had learnt. Omega was silenced.

'What have you been doing—you and Nan—to-day?' she asked, to change the subject.

'Doin'? What d'you s'pose? Nan and me don't do nothin'. We followed father to the pub, and he gave us both a drink. Didn't he, Nan?'

Nan nodded.

'It was so 'ot,' she said, 'and burnt me.'

'Brandy,' remarked Bill, shortly.

'And have you eaten nothing?' asked Omega.

'Mother gave Nan a crust——'

'Ah! and you have gone without! You are a little hero! There! go and buy something—mind, not drink!'

When Nan and Bill were gone, Omega took her baby in her arms, and, while it sucked at her breast, she sang the refrain of an old song. Of a sudden, she caught sight of her face in the broken looking-glass above the mantel-shelf, and broke off abruptly. She gazed with amazement. What a change a few months had wrought! Sallow and careworn, it was no longer the face of a young woman. She gazed for a moment, then turned away in disgust.

The days wore on monotonously, and the child

grew; and Omega felt happier than she had felt for months. With Angharad to cheer her with her babyish laughter and babyish play, she was content to live in the present, and be happy.

But babies, like human beings in general, will not laugh and will not play on empty stomachs; and the day came when, consequent upon her mother's fasting, Angharad showed the reverse side of her disposition. She became fractious, and whined. Omega was in distress.

'What shall I do, my darling? You are hungry —and so am I.' She might have added, 'the land-lady, too, for her week's rent.'

In fact, as she soliloquised, Mrs. Johnson entered the room. She looked more gaunt and fierce than usual; for, in addition to the customary black eyes, her face was ornamented with a livid weal that crossed the left cheek. It was an additional proof of her husband's strong feeling for her. She advanced to the centre of the room, and stood there with arms folded, eyeing Omega sternly. As she showed no inclination to speak, Omega opened the conversation, though her heart was throbbing with alarm.

'Well, Mrs. Johnson,' she said.

'Ay, it is "Well, Mrs. Johnson!"' exclaimed the landlady, in a suspicious tone. 'Where's my rent? that's what I want to know!'

'I am very sorry——'

'What!' Mrs. Johnson's suspicions being verified, she spoke in a terribly harsh, strident voice. 'You are goin' to try and play me that trick, are you? Not if I know it! I'm no fool, and I don't look one, neither! Don't you think you can gammon me! I'm wide awake, I can tell you! There's no takin' me in! Now then!'

'What do you want of me?' asked Omega, meekly.

'My rent, o' course! Where is it?'

'I have no money——'

'Rubbish! You must get it!'

'I assure you——'

'Or, out you go!'

'Do not be hard on me—and my baby. Look at the darling. She wants nourishment; so do I. I would not lose her for the world. I should not know what to do if she left me. She is so pretty, so good. Have pity! Look at her. If she died, it would kill me. She is so much to me. You are good and kind, I feel sure. Be merciful!'

Mrs. Johnson answered this appeal by a contemptuous smile.

'You make me laugh. You know you can easily pay the rent, if you like.'

'Tell me how,' cried Omega.

'As if you don't know! You can't gull me with your affected simplicity. You are young, with a pretty face, much as mine was at your age. A girl with such an attractive face as yours can always get a living.'

Omega coloured deeply at the covert allusion, and sprang angrily to her feet; but, a moment later, she recollected her defenceless position, and sank quietly into a chair. Mrs. Johnson, perceiving that her shaft had sped home, turned to leave the room.

'Remember,' she said, as she paused by the door, 'I must have the rent to-morrow, or you and your little darling are bundled out into the street.'

When she was gone, Omega sat with her head buried in her hands in a kind of stupor, in which the brain works without producing thought—thinking, yet not thinking—until the baby's whining caught her ear.

She rose and cast her eyes round the room, and,

in doing so, caught sight of the brooch which she
had once offered to Sal. She uttered a cry of delight, and, laying Angharad safely on the bed, rushed
with it from the house.

It was her first introduction to a pawnbroker, and
she approached that dignitary with an amount of
respect which at once informed him of the kind of
person he had to deal with. He offered to advance
her a tithe of the value of the bauble, and she accepted it greedily. The poor and the unhappy we
have always with us—thank God, ye who grow
rich upon their misery!

Omega bought the food she needed, and paid her
rent, and for a time the dreaded day was staved
off.

But soon again she was in the same wretched
circumstances. The rent was in arrear, and the
baby cried. There was no lucky brooch this time.
What was she to do? She sat for a long time by
the bedside, with the pangs of hunger eating into
her vitals, considering the fearful step that Fate
almost forced her to take. It was night, and the
darkness was only relieved by a flickering flare from
the gas-lamp over the way. It was raining, and she
heard the raindrops beating against the window, and

the clear, ringing footsteps of the passers-by. There was a silence in the air—the traffic had ceased—and sounds from without came with strange clearness upon her ear. She heard a half-drunken man go by, singing merrily, until he began to abuse a lamp-post that had got in the way and knocked against him. She heard a little street-boy sauntering by, varying a shrill whistle with a cry of 'Lights! Lights!' until the harsh voice of a policeman stopped his whistle and started him off at a run.

She went to the window and looked out. The street was not inviting, yet it was the only place that offered her bread. Hearing her baby cry, she took down her hat and cloak, and donned them carelessly. The cry ceased, and she paused by the window. One more impulsion was necessary. It came—a long wail from Angharad. She sighed, and left the house.

CHAPTER V.

It has been seen that Charles, in order to gratify his whims, was compelled to lower his flag of superiority before Dick, and to adopt the humble tone of a suppliant. This proceeding was naturally distasteful to him, and he felt a great increase of bitterness towards his friend, which he was not always able to conceal. Dick had imposed no task of any kind upon him in return for the favour he had granted, nor had he shown any inclination to adopt any other than his usual deferential manner towards him ; yet Charles fancied that he could detect some slight alteration in his companion's voice, which seemed to him in his frame of mind to be peculiarly aggressive.

The first notion of any such alteration came to his mind a day or two after he had received the money, when he was engaged in a conversation with Dick, at which his new acquaintance, Pillbury, happened to be present. They were talking on ordinary topics, when Dick, turning to Charles, said :

'I hope, sir, you have been able to discharge your promise to the young lady you mentioned during our conversation the other day ?'

' What young lady ?' asked Charles haughtily. ' I never mentioned one.'

' Pardon me, sir,' said Dick, assuming his wonted smile, the excessive blandness of which always had an exasperating effect on Charles—'pardon me, sir, I remember it perfectly. I think I may guess that her name was Mandeville—Miss Topsie Mandeville, of the Variety.'

Charles twisted his moustache vigorously.

' Well, suppose it was—what then ?'

' Oh, nothing, sir, only I should be glad to know that she was not disappointed, and so would my friend Pillbury, I'm sure.'

' Indeed !'

Charles eyed Pillbury in a threatening manner, which made that reserved young gentleman feel quite uncomfortable.

' Oh yes. You see, sir,' continued Dick, ' he was partly the means of your getting the money.'

'How so?'

'Well, for one thing, he cashed the cheque I gave him.'

'Indeed!' sneered Charles. 'Such extraordinary service merits my warmest thanks.'

He bowed ironically to Pillbury, who blushed to the roots of his hair, and cast an appealing look at Dick.

'Don't you mind,' said the latter, encouragingly. 'Our friend here evidently doesn't know that even the mere cashing of a cheque is sometimes a more serious operation than it seems.' Then, observing that Charles was puzzled by the remark, he added, in the same smiling, composed manner, 'Though, of course, there's nothing very wonderful in it after all. It gives a little trouble ; but you are too good a fellow, Alf, to mind that when your friends are concerned.'

Pillbury coloured with satisfaction at this compliment, and exclaimed in one burst, 'Not in the least!'

'Possibly, Mr. Pillbury may have put me under an obligation,' said Charles, looking disdainfully at the object of his speech, 'but allow me to suggest that our acquaintance has been scarcely long enough for me to number him among my friends.'

'Mr. Pillbury, I am sure, has no pretensions at present to that honour, sir,' said Dick, with a sudden seriousness which made Charles eye him very keenly to detect any hidden meaning. 'Even I, who have known you so many years, and have served you so faithfully, have only lately been permitted to take my place among your friends. As an humble friend, of course, sir—a position I value above everything. As for you, Alf,' he continued, turning to Pillbury, 'you must not hope for such an honour upon so short an acquaintance. I should feel jealous of you if you obtained it. In four or five years, perhaps, if you are earnest, industrious, and properly deferential, you may aspire——'

'That'll do! That'll do!' cried Charles pettishly, under the impression that Dick was secretly laughing at him. 'I've got something else to do than to sit here listening to your long-winded speeches. I'm off.'

He rose from his seat, and put on his hat.

'To Miss Mandeville's?' asked Dick, blandly smiling.

'Perhaps so!' These words were accompanied by a look which plainly said, 'What the deuce is that to you?'

'Ah, sir,' said Dick, 'we shall be having you here again shortly for another cheque, I fancy. Take care, sir; Miss Mandeville is a mighty extravagant young lady.'

'Well, if she is, I shall have to come upon you all the sooner ; so you know what to expect.'

'All right, sir.   Mr. Pillbury and myself will use our best endeavours in your service, never fear.'

The time came much sooner than Charles had anticipated.   Miss Mandeville was a very rapacious young woman, and her admirers could only hope to retain her favour by making frequent votive offerings at her shrine—in St. John's Wood.   Being of a calculating disposition, she was anxious to secure an independence against the day when, her charms having fled, her admirers would naturally desert her;   and this anxiety led her to make constant demands on the purses of her male friends. Who can resist the pleadings of a fascinating little lady who vows that unless she possesses the object on which her heart is set, she will pine and fall ill —and worse, transfer her affections to another! Not Charles, at any rate, for he ceased not to gratify the young lady's whims while there was still money left to chink in his pocket.

When he applied again to Dick, he reminded him of his promise to provide further supplies, and begged him in the sacred name of friendship to let the amount be as large as possible. This second appeal was not, as the first was, attended with any feeling of wounded pride. The tone of the suppliant was becoming natural to him, and, so long as he got the money, he cared little what paths of degradation he might tread.

Probably, Dick felt pleased at this change of manner; for he readily admitted his promise, and, without any demur, assured Charles that the money should be at his disposal on the following day.

'Don't fear, sir,' he said. 'Pillbury and myself will have no difficulty in getting the money. In fact, I've been rather lucky in my speculations lately, and I can therefore afford to deal generously towards you. Come at twelve o'clock to-morrow, and you will find Pillbury here with the money.'

Charles went away elated, and spent the evening so joyously, that it was past two o'clock when he arrived on the following day at Deadmen's Court. Dick was waiting there for him with an unpleasant surprise.

' I am sorry, sir,' he said, in a grave tone, ' but I am afraid you will have to do without the money. Pillbury hasn't turned up; something has happened to him.   He won't come now.'

' But I must absolutely have this money,' said Charles, anxiously.   ' It is most important.'

' That may be, sir; but you must try and get along without it—that's certain.'

' I can't, I tell you !   You promised me——'

' I relied on Pillbury.'

' What has he got to do with it ?   You told me yourself that he was a mere tool in your hands.'

' Very true ; but he's gone.'

' Gone where ?'

' That I can't say.'

  With the money ?'

Dick smiled for the first time.

' I hardly think, sir, that he was allowed to get it.'

' Allowed ?   You speak in riddles.   But come, understand me ; I must have this money, or——'

' Or what, sir ?'

' I shall cut my connection with you.'

' Would that be fair, sir ?   I have served you without payment; I have supplied you with money——'

'To remind me of these services is about the worst way to get me to repay them. Can you do me any more? That is the thing. If not, our acquaintance ends, and I am off.'

'Where?'

'Anywhere—to the devil, probably.'

He took up his hat and stick, and turned to the door. Dick stopped him.

'One moment, sir. Our acquaintance has existed too long to be cut short in this manner. You will excuse me, but I can't permit it. I have excellent reasons for what I say—I can't permit it.'

'Permit it!' exclaimed Charles fiercely.

'Yes, sir. We are too necessary for each other at this moment to part company. You can re-assure yourself, sir—you shall have the money.'

'You really mean it?'

'Yes—not to-day, to-morrow.'

Charles's passion quickly subsided under the soothing influence of this new promise. He apologized for his hasty expressions, and shook hands cordially with Dick at parting.

On the day following he again attended at Dead-men's Court, and found Dick seated at his desk by the window, with a cheque before him.

'No bad news to-day, I hope?'

'No, sir,' said Dick. 'You can have the money as soon as you wish. This cheque has been transferred to me in settlement of a bet, and only needs being cashed. It is for four hundred and fifty pounds. Two hundred will do for me, and you can keep the rest.'

Charles took the cheque in his hand, and examined it. It was drawn on the Metropolitan and Suburban Bank, and was made payable to a Mr. Samuel Gaythorpe, who had properly endorsed it.

'Am I to present it?' he asked.

'If you will, sir,' answered Dick. 'The bank is no distance from here, and you will be back in half an hour.'

Charles pondered for a moment to satisfy himself that there was nothing subservient in the mere act of presenting a cheque.

'Very well,' he said, 'but don't think, you know, that I am going to undertake any of Pillbury's duties.'

'Oh, no, sir!' cried Dick laughingly. 'There's no fear of that.'

Charles started off on his mission, and, having

safely accomplished it, returned to the presence of his friend, to whom he duly handed his share of the proceeds of the cheque. Dick received it with much satisfaction.

'This will keep us going for a time,' he said, 'and then I must get you to make another journey to the Bank.   Come, let us have a bottle together over it, and drink to the success of our new partnership.'

There was an approach to familiarity in these words which Charles did not like; but, with his money fresh in his pocket, he felt in no mood to be easily affronted, and accepted Dick's proposition with a very plausible heartiness.

CHAPTER VI.

THE Professor had, as already stated, two important objects in coming to town. One was to discover, if possible, the whereabouts of his unfortunate child ; while the other was to arrange for the publication of the earlier part of his long-meditated work.

The Professor, in his childlike simplicity, had never attempted to think out the means by which he might attain his first object; and, consequently, when the time came for acting he was obliged to pause and set his brains to work to conceive a plan. This proved to be a hopeless task, though he taxed his mind to the utmost; and had he been left to his own resources, his search after Omega would never have been begun. But his friend Phillips came gallantly to his rescue, and, with his practical sense, quickly solved the difficulty.

'If you were to walk about the streets every day from noon till night,' he said, 'it is possible that you might eventually come across her; but the odds are so great against the success of such a plan, that you may as well dismiss it at once from your mind. No, no, old boy; we'll try a plan rather different from that, which ought to succeed if she is in London. We'll just circulate among the different police-stations a full description of her, offering a small reward for any information leading to her discovery. What do you say to that?'

'It is certainly ingenious,' remarked the Professor; 'but the—the publicity——'

'Nonsense! No one but the police will know of it, and yours, you may be sure, will be only one out of dozens of such cases in their hands. Leave it to me. It shall be done, and, if she is in London, you shall have her in your arms again within six weeks.'

The Professor readily assented upon being assured that he would not have to undergo the mortification of beholding printed bills referring to his daughter stuck up in all the thoroughfares, and left the affair wholly in Phillips's hands. Within a week every police-station in London was supplied with a full description of a girl named Omega Hewitson, and all the men were instructed, in case she should be met with, to follow her and take down her address. This was excellently done, and reflected credit on Phillips's ingenuity; only, it fell short in one particular—in omitting all mention of the circumstances under which she had left her home. Had these been known, the police, with their knowledge of the ways of young women in her condition, would have been better armed for the undertaking. Thus it happened that the six weeks so glibly spoken of by Phillips, and many more, went quickly by without the smallest trace of the missing girl being obtained. The Professor allowed the first two or three months to pass without any diminution of his hopeful feeling; then, as day by day glided by without any news of his daughter, his faith in the efficacy of Phillips's plan became gradually extinguished, and he at length seemed to have banished all thoughts of her from his mind.

In this state of things he gladly turned to the prosecution of his other object, and found plenty of occupation in preparing the earlier portion of his work for the press.

'A part is better than none,' said Phillips encouragingly.

'To be sure!' cried the Professor joyously, and he went to work with great ardour.

But even in the pet project of his life, malignant Fate was pursuing him, and endeavouring to bring the labour of so many years to nought. Whilst Phillips was reading the newspaper in the Professor's room one day, he suddenly gave a start, and, in his agitation, let his pipe drop from his mouth. The Professor was seated at his desk, arranging the sheets of his MS., and was placidly labouring to drive a pin without a point through a number of them. He lifted his eyes on hearing the noise of the fallen pipe, and glanced through his spectacles at his friend. Phillips was deadly pale, and avoided his glance nervously.

'What is it, friend Phillips,' asked the Professor, 'that has startled you so?'

Phillips bent down to pick up his pipe, and at the same time to hide his tell-tale face, and murmured, 'Nothing—nothing.'

The Professor was not satisfied with this answer, and directed his eyes so that they should meet Phillips's when the latter's face was raised. His strategy was rewarded; Phillips coloured like a peony, and looked quickly away.

'Ah, Phillips, I see there is something that you wish to conceal from me; but I am too sharp for you. Come, tell me what it is.'

Phillips, having regained his composure, put his pipe in his mouth for answer, and smoked defiantly.

'You must be aware,' continued the Professor, 'that there is very little use in concealing anything from me. I am sure to learn it from some other source.'

The smoke rose from Phillips's pipe in rapidly succeeding clouds.

'I am not curious by nature,' resumed the Professor, 'at least not impertinently curious; and were I not assured that you have some intelligence—probably of a serious character—directly concerning me, I should make no attempt to induce you to speak.'

Puff! puff! in quick succession; the room was filling with smoke.

The Professor felt hurt at his friend's determined silence, and, rising in his chair, eyed him for a few moments with great solemnity. This silent protest meeting with no result, he sat down again, and, waving his bandanna at Phillips, exclaimed in a tone of much dignity:

'I am sorry, indeed, that, after a friendship existing for so many years, you should withdraw your confidence from me. I am not sensible of having deserved it; but if I have been guilty of aught——'

He paused here to cough, when Phillips, touched by his companion's words, burst forth into an explanation.

'My good old friend, do you think for a moment that I would conceal anything from you, unless I feared that it might affect your happiness! If you will have an explanation, I can only say that I have read a paragraph in this d——d paper——'

'My dear Phillips!'

'Well! Read it, yourself! I won't read it again! It's scandalous! After the labour of so many years! To be forestalled! I say the fellow ought to be locked up, and his printed trash burnt by the common hangman! He must have learnt your intention, be hanged to him for a dirty, dishonourable scoundrel!'

'My dear Phillips,' exclaimed the Professor, 'what is the matter? You are talking in enigmas.'

'Read! Read! There!'

Phillips banged the paper into the Professor's hands, and dashed his pipe down on the table. The Professor, astonished at his friend's outburst of

temper, looked at him for a moment in alarm ; and
then, anxious to learn the cause of such an unusual
display, directed his eye to the paragraph indicated.

This is what he saw :

IN PREPARATION.

THE GREEK TRAGIC POETS: THEIR LIVES AND THEIR WORKS.

BY THEOPHILUS O'GRADY.

In 2 Vols., Crown 8vo.

TOMPSON & CO., PUBLISHERS, GREAT DUKE STREET, W.

The Professor folded the paper up, and laid it
quietly on the table. Not a word did he utter, but,
as he leaned back in his chair, he gave vent to a
long-drawn sigh. Phillips saw the necessity for
consolation.

'What does it matter, after all ?' he said, with an
affected laugh. 'There is plenty of room for two
such works, and, though his may have a start, yours,
when it appears, will swallow his up. Who is he, I
should like to know ?'

'That I cannot tell you,' said the Professor gently;
' but he could not have dealt me a heavier blow
had he been my most inveterate enemy. The
labour of so many years—to be forestalled after
all !'

'Stuff! rubbish!' cried Phillips, forgetting that the Professor was merely repeating words which he had used a few moments before. 'Nothing of the kind! His book, I'll be bound, is only a catchpenny thing. It will serve as a whet to yours—like a few oysters before a good, solid dinner.'

'I wish I could think so,' said the Professor.

Phillips was silent for a while, and then jumped to his feet.

'By Jove! I've an idea! We'll go and see a publisher at once, and see whether we can't beat this fellow, after all. We'll try Bradys—first-class publishers; none of your Tompson and Co.'s for us. Come along, come along; don't let us lose a moment!'

The Professor was infected with his friend's spirit, and rose from his chair.

'You are right, my dear Phillips, you are right. We will have no delay. Come, then.'

He gathered up the MS. before him, and made it into a parcel. It was rather bulky, but the Professor felt no inconvenience from its weight. He placed it tenderly under his left arm, and followed Phillips from the room.

Within a short time they found themselves seated

in a draughty, ill-furnished room, in company with a sharp, intelligent young man, who, like many others of his generation, had hurried at such a pace through life, that he had worn away almost the whole of the natural covering of his head. A strange incongruity, yet not uncommon in these busy days—a fresh, young face surmounted by a bald pate. Such belonged to 'our Mr. Brady junior.'

The Professor and Phillips were both rather intimidated by his dashing, business manner.

'Sit down, sit down!' he said, with a hasty wave of his hand as they entered, a command—for it sounded very like one — which the two friends obeyed by seating themselves noiselessly in an obscure corner, with their hats on their knees.

'One moment, gentlemen,' continued Mr. Brady junior, 'I shall be at your service.'

With this, he dashed to a speaking-tube, and hurled up some terribly obscure remarks; then skipped to another and did likewise, and, after skirmishing round the room, plumped into a chair.

The two friends followed his movements with startled eyes and bated breath, and felt as schoolboys feel when making the acquaintance of a new pedagogue.

'Now, then,' cried Mr. Brady junior, eyeing them keenly, 'I am at liberty. Your business, gentlemen.'

The Professor turned to Phillips, and whispered, 'You had better explain,' to which Phillips responded by ejaculating a sonorous 'Hem!' followed by a long pause.

'I am waiting, gentlemen,' said Mr. Brady junior.

The Professor grasped his MS. firmly, and began :

'The fact is, sir, that I have been engaged for some years past in the production of a work——'

'A work of the highest merit!' exclaimed Phillips, encouraged by the sound of his friend's voice, 'and one which ought to startle the world!'

'Yes ?'

'My friend,' continued the Professor, 'is pleased to speak highly of its merits, whether or no with justice it is not for me to say. You are a publisher, I believe ?'

Mr. Brady junior nodded his head.

'Then, sir, I should be glad if we could enter into an arrangement for the publication of my work— an arrangement, I mean, whereby you would undertake to do whatever is necessary to bring it before the public, recouping yourself out of the profits derived from its sale.'

'A certain fortune for a publisher!' exclaimed Phillips.

'I have the MS. with me,' continued the Professor, holding it modestly up to view. 'If you would like——'

'What's it about?' asked Mr. Brady junior abruptly.

'It treats of the works of the great tragic poets of Greece——'

'A finer subject couldn't be found!' cried Phillips.

'It is, in short,' continued the Professor, 'an exhaustive commentary on the Greek stage of that period, and is illustrated by very copious translations.'

'And you want us to publish it at our own risk?' exclaimed Mr. Brady junior, with a smile. 'It's no go, gentlemen. You'd better try elsewhere.'

'I beg your pardon?' said the Professor, in an incredulous tone.

'I say it's no go!' cried Mr. Brady junior, with increased sharpness. 'There's no demand for

such heavy works. We were had over a " Plato"
only a short time ago—quite against my wish we
undertook it. D——n Plato, I say!'

The Professor looked at him aghast, while Phillips
began to colour with anger.

'The public won't read such stuff nowadays,
They want something light. Sorry I can't oblige
you. Good-day, gentlemen.'

The Professor felt sick at heart.

'Surely,' he began, 'there is always a sufficient
public——'

'No, no. They won't read anything deep. If
you could write a smart novel—something light
and laughable—then perhaps——'

Phillips bounded to his feet, and his pent-up rage
burst forth.

'Do you mean to insult us? This gentleman's
work is worth a hundred of your cursed light
novels! Something laughable, indeed! Why, confound
it! do you think this gentleman, who knows ten
times more than you and I put together, would
condescend to make an idiotic public laugh?'

'Gently, Phillips, gently!' put in the Professor.

'There is the door, gentlemen,' said Mr. Brady
junior, with a wave of his hand. 'You must excuse

me. I can't discuss the matter. Good-day.' And he bounded from his chair, and began shouting fresh commands up the speaking-tube.

The Professor laid his hand gently on Phillips's shoulder, to restrain him from further venting his anger; and, having succeeded, he replaced his MS. under his arm, and, preceded by his friend, slowly passed out of the room.

As they walked down the street, neither addressed the other, but both dropped occasional exclamations indicative of their feelings towards the shrewd young gentleman whose presence they had just quitted—from the mild 'Silly fellow!' of the Professor to the forcible 'D——d insulting rascal!' of Phillips.

The Professor endeavoured to hide his dejection from his friend, and presently, when they had reached the bottom of the street, took him to task for wasting his anger on so foolish a fellow.

'Come, come, Phillips,' he said; 'all is not lost. There are other publishers, I believe, in this large city. They cannot all be such shallow-brained persons as the young man whom we have just left. We must not despair at the first rebuff.'

But in his heart he experienced that benumbing

feeling which many a man has known when a long-cherished hope—conceived amidst bright visions, and developed with all the fervour of an absorbing passion—has suddenly to be abandoned as a vain, foolish illusion.

CHAPTER VII.

Timeo Danaos et dona ferentes. If Charles had
been a scholar, this old maxim might have recalled
itself to his mind, and given rise to some reflection
in the matter of his dealings with his friend Dick.
He might have asked himself whether it was
natural that a man whom he had always treated as
a very inferior being should be willing to render
him benefits without any intention of exacting
payment in the manner most satisfactory to himself.
But Charles was no scholar—only a thoughtless,
reckless prodigal, intent upon getting the maximum
of pleasure from life, and careless how much it
might ultimately cost him.

Yet it is not quite the fact to say that he was
free from suspicion that Dick's generosity was not
altogether prompted by the blind desire to administer to his wants and free him from his em-
barrassments. He felt that Dick must have some

hidden object; but his pecuniary needs on the one hand, and his careless disposition on the other, prevented him from sufficiently considering it to arrive at an idea of its true nature.

Nor were there wanting signs of warning which should have put him on his guard. He saw them and recognised them, and vented bitter curses on his companion's head; but paid no further heed to them. He remarked the tone of familiarity which Dick had of late adopted in place of the subservient tone of old. The 'Sir' had been quietly dropped, and he was made to feel that the relation in which they stood towards each other was that of man and man, no longer that of master and servant. This change of manner was exceedingly galling to his pride; but Charles submitted to it in the knowledge that it was the price—perhaps only a part of the price—which he had to pay for the services rendered to him. He made no protests in Dick's presence, though his scowling brow and clenched jaw were very patent signs of his inward feelings.

Another grievance of his—though scarcely a reasonable one—was that he had always to cash the cheques which fed his and Dick's wants. On one occasion he objected, observing 'that he hadn't bargained to run errands.'

Dick's answer was short.

'Then you can't have the money.'

'Why don't you cash the cheque yourself?' asked Charles.

'Because I prefer you to.'

'Where's Pillbury? Why don't you get him to do it?'

Dick laughed lightly.

'He's too much engaged—and will be, I expect, for the next year or eighteen months.'

Charles ground his teeth together, and cursed Dick liberally in his heart, but made no further objection.

Thus, with the progress of time, the hatred of Charles for his old servant and playfellow grew deeper and deeper. It had not reached a culminating point as yet, but that period was not far off.

One day, within a few months of his protest against his employment as Dick's messenger, he made a discovery. He was sitting down in Miss Mandeville's boudoir, and, while waiting for that young lady's appearance, was turning over a file of newspapers of recent date. He was reading a paragraph here and a paragraph there in a careless manner, when his attention was arrested by meeting with the name of ' Alfred Pillbury.'

He drew the paper nearer to him, and read as follows :

' Alfred Pillbury, aged 22, was on Tuesday last indicted at the Central Criminal Court for uttering a forged cheque on the 10th of August last, knowing the same to be forged. The cheque itself was perfectly genuine, excepting as to the amount, which had been by the aid of chemicals most ingeniously altered from the original amount of £3 15s. to £315. The prisoner urged in his defence that he was unaware that the cheque was forged, and that he merely presented it at the request of another man, whose name, however, he refused to divulge. The Judge, in summing up, observed that it was very possible that the prisoner was a mere tool in the hands of a more designing man, but that such a plea could not exempt him from the consequences of association with men of criminal habits. The prisoner was found guilty, and was sentenced to eighteen months' imprisonment.'

Charles felt so dazed after the first perusal, that he read the paragraph over again to assure himself that he perfectly understood its import. There could be no doubt about it ; the man whom poor Pillbury refused to betray was none other than Dick Revell, who, having lost his first tool, was seeking for another in the person of Charles himself. He turned hot and cold alternately, and, for the first time in his life, was attacked by a nervous feeling of dread.

Could he hope to break off his connection with Dick ? Had he not gone too far to attempt to free himself ? Had he not allowed himself to sink too deep into the mire to extricate himself ? Was he not hopelessly within his enemy's power ? Could he not feel his fatal influence closing upon him— as the tentacles of an octopus close upon the drowning fisherman—whence there could be no escape ?

But these unpleasant fears soon left him, and gave place to a fit of inward rage as he thought how completely he had been outwitted by his astute companion. He, who prided himself upon his cunning, and fancied that no one could overreach him, had been a mere plastic instrument in the hands of a man who had been bred up as a help in a stable.

He had allowed this upstart to proceed steadily and deliberately in his purpose—without attempting to fathom it or to counteract it—until he found him-self converted into a mere puppet, to move and act according to another's bidding—and that other a former dependant !

These degrading thoughts worked Charles into a fury, and he determined to lose no time in confront-ing his enemy, and pouring out the vials of his anger upon him. He cut out the paragraph refer-ring to Pillbury, and, having left a little note giving Miss Mandeville sufficient reasons for his strange departure, hurried off at full speed to Deadmen's Court.

He ascended the stairs quickly, and burst into the room, intending to take Dick unawares. He found him—as on a former occasion—seated by the window, with the contents of the tin box scattered about on the table before him, and on the desk a cheque undergoing manipulation. He expected that Dick would turn pale and endeavour to hide the traces of his work, or would at any rate show the trepidation natural in a man detected in the commission of a criminal act. But no; Dick merely gave one quick glance at him, as though to note the state of his feelings, and then calmly proceeded with his work.

Charles was staggered for a moment by this marvellously cool demeanour, and watched Dick in angry amazement; but he speedily recovered himself, and strode fiercely forward until he stood immediately facing his adversary.

'I have found you out at last!' he cried, in a passionate voice.

'Indeed!'

Dick looked up with a calm, unruffled face as he uttered this exclamation, and then looked down again. He was using a crow-quill pen, and Charles, in spite of his excitement, could not help noting that the hand guiding it showed not the slightest quiver of agitation.

'You have tried to deceive me,' he cried, 'but you have failed! That poor tool of yours, Pillbury, where is he? Tell me!'

Dick raised his eyes again calmly, and, with a provoking smile, said:

'You know where he is.'

'Yes, I do!' exclaimed Charles fiercely; 'I do know where he is!'

'Then why ask me?'

This retort, delivered in the most placid manner, increased Charles's irritation, but arrested for the moment his flow of speech. Dick's attitude was so unexpected, that it quite drove out of his head the elaborate denunciation that had been shaping itself in his mind.

'You are willing to admit where he is now that I have found it out,' he said, after a short pause. 'The poor fool is lodged in prison; while you, who instigated him, are at liberty.'

'That is so,' said Dick, laying his pen down in anticipation of a sharp verbal combat.

'You made no attempt to save him!'

'What could I do? He was taken in the act, and no action of mine——'

'Enough! You sicken me with your excuses!'

'You haven't given me time to make any yet.'

'You can make none! You have played a low, blackguardly part.'

'I deny it.'

'It is true!' cried Charles, bringing his fist down furiously on the desk. 'I say you are a coward— a mean, pitiful coward, who ought to be kicked from one end of London to the other! How dare you put yourself forward as a gentleman — a mean, low cad, with the breeding and tastes of a gallows-bird! You thought to outwit me—to force yourself upon me as an equal! You—a dirty, white-livered coward, who desert your friends at the first sign of danger !'

'That is false,' said Dick quietly.

'It is not! This poor fool, Pillbury, by whom you benefited——'

'And you too. Don't forget that.'

'If I had known where you got the money from, do you think I would have touched it ?'

'I don't think you would have been very particular, so long as you did get it.'

'It's a lie !' cried Charles, with flashing eyes. 'However badly off I might be, I would never accept money at the hands of a miserable sneak who betrays his friends——'

'Come, come !' said Dick, in an authoritative manner; 'we've had enough of calling names. Whatever I am, you know you must put up with me. If I can't turn myself into a gentleman to be your companion, you must turn yourself into a cad to become mine.'

He rose as he finished the sentence, and leisurely began to gather up the materials on the desk.

Charles was thunderstruck at the import conveyed in these words, which was indeed too plain to be missed. He, however, plucked up his courage, and played what he believed to be the most powerful card in his hand.

'What if I were to intimate to the authorities that a certain Mr. Dick Revell, who lives in Dead-men's Court, is the person who should suffer imprisonment in the place of poor Pillbury?'

Dick shrugged his shoulders.

'You were just blaming me for betraying my friends,' he said. 'It seems you, too, are not incapable of it.'

Charles smiled grimly; he fancied the trick was his.

'The cases are different. You are a mere common forger—a criminal of the lowest description. I should be doing a service to the country.'

'Surely,' said Dick, looking Charles straight in the face—'surely an accomplice ought to be the last person to betray his partner—if only for his own sake.'

Charles felt like one shot. He had to gulp down something in his throat before he could speak.

'An accomplice! Do you mean me?'

'Certainly,' answered Dick, with a light laugh. 'I draw the cheques—or forge them, if you like it better—and you utter them. So you see we are bound to each other by pretty strong ties; for, if one plays false to the other, the result is we both suffer. You must take care of yourself, now that you know of poor Pillbury's disaster. I can't afford to lose you, my dear fellow.'

Charles was leaning against the wall, pale and faint, listening to Dick's words without any sign of emotion.

'This is your revenge, then?' he said, in low grating tones, when Dick finished.

'For what?' asked Dick airily.

'I don't know for what—unless because I have been your master.'

'Oh no! I am not such an idiot as that! To be sure, you have sometimes given yourself tremendous airs, and have been exceedingly offensive; but one cannot expect to go through the world without meeting with some rubs. Besides, you were my master then, and had a certain right to be offensive. But that is all over now; we are man and man now, and stand upon a common platform. You have, indeed, been rather offensive to-day, but then you didn't thoroughly understand your position. You do now ; so it won't happen again.   Oh no ! I am not so foolish as to remember such trifles, though I admit you have stung me at times, and your condescension was occasionally a little too strong. But I was only a servant then, and you were my master.   It's different now.   No, no ! I wanted a good, useful fellow, with not too much principle, to help me— that's all.'

' To make a tool of him ?'

Dick laughed.

' Well, if you prefer the expression—yes.'

Charles ground his teeth together with suppressed rage.

' I am obliged to you for this explanation,' he said, with feigned calmness. ' Now I shall know exactly how I stand, and what is expected of me. But you must be careful how you use your tool. There is a certain limit of endurance ; take care that you do not pass it. If you are wise, you will keep this in memory. You will excuse me now, unless you have any commands for me. No ? Then good-day.'

He made a ceremonious bow to Dick, who returned it by a good-humoured nod of the head, and, walking firmly to the door, descended into the street.

CHAPTER VIII.

THE downward road is an easy one. It is straight and broad, and its descent is so exquisitely graduated that you progress with marvellous speed. You obey the laws of gravity; you begin by walking, and end by running. You are able at first to look round and survey your position; afterwards the motion is too hurried—you cannot stop if you wish.

This is the road on which Omega was travelling with all a woman's recklessness. In a woman, loss of virtue—though more frequently than not the result of a deep and earnest love that can refuse nothing—is equivalent to the loss of every moral quality. A man may make many slips before he loses his position; one is enough in a woman. Society points the finger of scorn at her, and her doom is sealed. She retires from the world's gaze in shame; then rebels, and casts off her shame. Her time is short; she outrages nature, and falls an early

victim to death. She has travelled by the downward road.

It is unnecessary to enter into particulars of the
life of a poor woman who journeys by this road;
suffice it that Omega made more ravages upon her
constitution in six months than she had done in all
the previous years of her life put together. She had
lost, too, the most ordinary womanly qualities, such
as cleanliness, modesty, and sobriety. She had
become reckless, and had learnt a new language that
matched her conduct. She had almost passed beyond the point when kind, gentle treatment could
rescue her; she was depraved—almost beyond hope
of redemption.

In spite of neglect and dirt, Angharad throve, and,
at a year old, was a strong and healthy baby. With
her other virtues, Omega's maternal love had deserted her, and Angharad experienced the seamy
side of life even before she had learnt to speak her
wants. She had a very hard time of it now and
then from the neglectful conduct of her mother, and,
had not Providence sent her a protector, it is doubt-
ful whether she would have lived to see one anni-
versary of her birthday. This protector was young
in years and judgment; he belonged to the male

sex, and dressed usually in rags. His name was Bill, and he had a dependent sister, named Nan.

It may be asked, What stirred this precocious lad's humanity in favour of the youthful Angharad? He had more than once expressed his contempt for babies, and, in Nan, had already sufficiently burdened himself with responsibilities. Well, for one thing, he remembered Omega's kindness; and, for another, it added to his self-importance to have two dependants instead of one. As usual, benevolence had its source in two motives—love of fellow-men and love of self.

For her part, Angharad soon came to look upon him as a providential substitute for her mother, and surrendered to him her young and tender affections. When he was in the room, her eyes would seek his with an appealing look, and she would crawl along the ground to find shelter in his arms. These proofs of her regard and respect Bill received with a pleased condescension. He brought her strange and tasty things to eat, purchased with her mother's money, and carried her occasionally with him into the street. But to prevent any unbecoming familiarity, he habitually addressed her in a loud, authoritative

tone, calling her by the strangest and most undigni-
fied appellations.

'Now then, young sprat,' he would say, 'I'm a-goin'
to take you out with me. Ain't I a brick, eh ? Just
let Nan hoist you on my shoulder. There you are,
my little crockerydile. Now, off we goes, and mind
you behaves yourself, or else I'll give you a rope's-
end when we comes back.' Which threat, however,
did not prevent Angharad from crowing with happiness.

Omega saw little of her two old friends, Sal and
Mary Ann ; in fact, they had had a serious quarrel.
It arose in respect of a certain trifling amount which
Omega had handed to Mary Ann for the purpose
of getting some gin for general consumption in the
house. Mary Ann had returned without the gin,
but with a very plausible story, from which it
appeared that the coin had slipped from her hand
and had rolled down a grating. But as there was a
strong odour of the fiery liquor about her, her story
was discredited by Omega, and a dispute began
which ended in her formally declining all further
acquaintance with either Sal or Mary Ann. There
was ingratitude in this act, considering the many
deeds of kindness that she had experienced at their

hands; but, as has been shown, the Omega of old was no longer in existence.

She lived a miserable, solitary life, that was far worse than death itself. She seldom or never thought of her troubles now; she was no longer haunted by horrible recollections: her brain was in a state of stupor. Once only did she recur to her former self. She was going out, and, by mere force of habit, turned to the looking-glass. She gave but one glance at her cruelly altered features, and then struck the glass so fiercely that it fell, shivered into fragments.

Her frame of mind made her submit quietly to her existence. She was content to continue it, careless whether Fortune had changes in store for her or not, a proof of how little is required to force humanity back into the mere animal stage of existence.

At length an event happened which compelled her to have recourse to her almost disused reasoning faculties. Mrs. Johnson, the landlady, so frequently woke her lodgers up with the cries she uttered during her marital disputes, that it came to be regarded as a matter of course that her voice should be heard in the night, and the awakened

sleepers simply cursed her very heartily, and turned
over in their beds to seek repose again.   But one
night it happened that her shrieks were hushed
almost immediately, and the morning sun, as it
broke feebly into the room, found her stretched
lifeless on the floor, with her husband calmly sleeping away the effects of yesterday's drink by her
side.   It was found that her skull had been beaten
in in half a dozen places, and a slight examination
of her husband's boots plainly indicated that they
were responsible for the indentations.   Was he
responsible himself?   He had no recollection of any
quarrel between them, having been in drink at the
time; but he readily admitted that doubtless a
quarrel had occurred, and that he had administered
what he considered retributive punishment. Surely
no British jury would hang a man for having
kicked his wife to death in a fit of drunken passion!
Where were an Englishman's boasted liberties if he
mightn't do what he liked with his own?   He was
an Englishman, had never done a stroke of work in
his life, had got drunk daily with his wife's earn-
ings, and had at last ended her existence by a
chance kick.   It was such a usual thing that no
one could regard it as a crime!   Besides, he was

sorry to lose her, though she had a confoundedly aggravating tongue. Excellent excuses in their way, but not yet sufficient to satisfy Justice.

When Bill was informed of the tragedy, he proved himself a thorough chip of the old block. He shed no tears; he expressed no sorrow; he merely said, while looking at his mother's corpse:

'What did she go a-aggerivatin' 'im for? As if any man would stand it from his wife! She ought to 'ave known she'd catch it!'

The death of this woman had a consequence which affected Omega as well as the other lodgers. The owner of the house, with that disregard of legal forms which can be employed with impunity in dealing with the very poor, turned them into the street. He gave no reason; it was his will—that had to be sufficient.

Thus Omega, one morning, found herself again houseless, with not only Angharad on her hands, but also Bill and Nan, who expressed their determination to share her fortunes. This new situation obliged her to bring her mind once more into play.

Omega led the way from the old lodging, followed by Bill bearing Angharad, and holding Nan by the hand. Omega looked serious, Bill adven-

turous, Angharad delighted, and Nan careless. The
expedition headed down the Westminster Road,
stopping a moment at the public-house at the
corner, to partake of liquid refreshment.

'Where are we goin' to ?' asked Bill.

'Anywhere,' replied Omega.

'That'll suit me. You hear, you young Buster !
We're goin' anywhere. Why don't yer laugh ?'

Angharad crowed, and pulled his hair.

'Hi, hi! cockey! Don't pull my feathers out!
Chuck it up, I tell you, or I'll warm you ! D'you
see that cove in blue ? He's a peeler. Thinks a
mighty lot of hisself, he does. He and me ain't
pals ; we've fallen out.   We don't speak, we don't ;
we ain't on friendly terms.   He'd do well for a
waxwork show, or a weather-cock on a chimley.
He's afraid of me, he is ; thinks I'll take 'is number, and summon 'im afore 'is hinspector. Now
then, who are you a-shovin' against ?' This was to
a youth of about his own age, who was balancing a
heavy parcel on his head.   'Go on with yer, or I'll
put you in the gutter, and sit on yer ! Go on,
ugly mug, or I shall hurt yer ! Yah! Hullo
Where are we ?'

They were passing down the Borough Road.

'All right! Go on. Who's afraid? That's a church, that is. People goes and sits in it, and kicks up a row a-singin'! I've seed 'em at it. Hold yer head up, Nan; you ain't tired yet. No, you ain't! If you says you is, I'll spank yer! Hullo, what's the row, my young squeecher? Oh, you see the oranges over there, do yer? Wouldn't you like one! Yes, don't you wish you may get it! Shut up your row! You'll 'ave the peeler after you. Look at the sodger! Ain't he fine! I shall be a sodger—perhaps—and go an' fight, an' kill no end of people. What are you a-doin' of?' This was to a middle-aged man, who had playfully touched him with his stick. 'You're a pretty one, ain't yer? Look like a goriller out for a 'oliday! Wonder what you'd fetch at a pawnshop! You'd frighten a cat, you would! Go on! Yah!'

Omega turned down a by-street.

'Hullo! Off we goes again! Well, my young cockywax, what are you a-thinkin' of? Do you know you're 'eavy? I shall drop you presently on the pavement, and smash you. Serve you right, wouldn't it? I ain't yer father, you know, though you may think I am. What are you doin'? Don't go a-kissin' of me! Who asked you to? Chuck it

up, and sit still, or I'll let you drop, I will, on yer
head.   Hullo!'

Omega had paused before a dirty, begrimed
house, having a board projecting forward, on which
was written the words, 'Bedrooms to let, from
2s. 6d. a week.'

'Come,' she said, turning to her following, 'this
will do.'

The expedition entered the house, and, an arrangement being speedily made, was soon enjoying
a rest from its labours.

Once more assured of a roof over her head, Omega
fell back into the blind state of life that had become so natural to her.   She cared for nothing—
she hoped for nothing; so long as she could gratify
her cravings, she was content to live.   She had
become terribly improvident, and, had it not been
for little Bill's prudent action in easing her of her
money on every possible occasion, the rent would
have fallen in arrear, and the children themselves
would have starved.   Gin, which before was merely
a slave, had become her master.   This led to a new
experience.

One evening she left the public-house in a daze,
and, after a few awkward steps, fell prone on the

pavement. She attempted to rise, but failed, and sank back helplessly. A crowd gathered round her, and passed jeering remarks, which she heard without understanding. Presently a policeman looked over the shoulders of the crowd, and asked, ' What was up ?'

' A woman—drunk,' was the laughing reply.

The representative of the law walked to her side, and attempted to raise her.

' Now then; up with you !'

Her answer was an inarticulate sound.

By dint of exertion, the constable at length raised her to her feet, and, with the aid of another of his body, conveyed her to the police-station. She was allowed to go away the next morning, after having received a severe caution from the Inspector. How could he have suspected that this wretched woman was the ' Omega Hewitson ' whose description was at the very moment lying within his desk ?

This experience—rough as it was—had no quieting effect upon her. Relying thoroughly upon little Bill for all necessary household management, she gave up her whole time to self-gratification. Such an arrangement could not be of long duration, even under far better conditions; in this instance it came to an end owing to an altogether unlooked-for circumstance.

Bill found it a more difficult task each week to draw supplies from Omega. He had to pass from request to entreaty, from entreaty to demand, from demand to theft. One day even theft was of no avail, for there was nothing to steal. She had spent her last penny to appease her craving for drink, and had returned home with just sufficient consciousness to lay herself down on the bed before sleeping. Angharad, fortunately, was asleep; but Nan was making the most indecent manifestations of her desire to fill up the vacuum inside her. Bill himself experienced an unpleasant sensation, which he could not get rid of even by trying to persuade himself that it was yesterday's crust undergoing the process of digestion. This uncomfortable feeling continuing, and Nan's ejaculations increasing, he rose from his seat, and calling upon his sister to accompany him, led the way into the street. Taking her hand in his, he paced along the pavements, every now and then appealing to a passer-by to give him a penny to buy bread.

Many of the strangers whom he accosted were good-hearted, benevolent men, who subscribed liberally to the orthodox charities with incomes as big as a prince's, but who could not bring themselves to bestow a penny on two ragged little beggars, who would not take a gruff answer, but ran by their sides until forcibly driven away. They acted not from indifference, but from pure disbelief in the idea that two beings could be near starvation in the great, wealthy metropolis. While there are such crowds of little waifs and strays amongst us—to many of whom, undoubtedly, the procuring of a meal presents anxious thoughts—it is perhaps as well for us to take our penny-pieces from our pockets, and chance whether they are deservedly given or not.

Being unsuccessful in meeting with a response to his appeals, Bill grew impatient, and resolved upon a bold course. He entered a baker's shop, and, under pretence of asking the price of a cake in the window, whisked two rolls from the counter under his coat. He performed this act with sufficient adroitness to blind the baker, but he had not taken into consideration that it might be observed from the street. He was therefore considerably surprised when the policeman whom he had alluded to in so jocular a fashion a few days previously stepped into the shop and laid a hand on his shoulder.

Bill struggled with all his might, and bit and scratched like a wild-cat, but his strength was soon exhausted, and he lay panting on the floor.

'Come 'ere!' he gasped, addressing Nan, who had entered the shop behind the policeman. 'The coppers have got us—I couldn't help it—p'r'aps they won't part us. 'Ere! see that loaf in the corner—no one's looking—go and swaller it—I don't want none!'

Nan and he were destined never again to see Omega. They were in due course brought before a magistrate, charged with being homeless and wandering aimlessly about the public streets, and were forthwith ordered to be delivered over to the tender mercies of a reformatory, for the several periods of five and seven years.

This was perhaps the best thing that could have happened to them; for, though it necessitated a parting, it gave each an opportunity of unlearning the cruel lessons of the past, and learning new lessons that might fit them to become useful citizens of their country.

CHAPTER IX.

IT may well be imagined that the candid explanation given to Charles by Dick did not tend to improve their mutual relationship. It is true that Dick made no alteration in his manner towards his companion, unless it were to make it more cheery and familiar; but Charles could not be brought to view the situation in the same amiable light.

His attitude towards Dick was that of a man who carries a volcano of rage within his breast, which is only prevented from bursting forth by the exertion of the utmost self-control. His pride had received a terrible chastisement. He had to bow to a man whom he regarded as the incarnation of a low, vulgar blackguard. He had to acknowledge this man, who had so successfully duped him, as a master whose commands he must perforce obey. This desperate feeling never abated, and it wanted only some great provocation that should break down his self-control to end in some desperate act. It seemed that he recognised this fact himself; for he made one attempt to work upon Dick's feelings to release him from his intolerable bondage.

They were seated together in the house in Dead-men's Court, when Charles spoke on the subject. He began in a calm, propitiatory tone, which sounded strange indeed to his companion.

'I have to ask a favour of you,' he said. 'I wish you to let me leave you. I am sure you can easily find a man more suited than I to help you in your schemes. I am worse than useless.'

'Not at all!' answered Dick smilingly. 'You suit me admirably. I am quite satisfied.'

'But the work is irksome to me. I am not fitted for it. You had better let me go. It would be a good thing for both of us.'

'How can you support yourself?' asked Dick. 'Where would your supplies come from ?'

'I should leave the country, or enlist.'

'Not a cheerful programme! You would soon be wishing you were back with me again, with plenty of money in your pockets, and little to do but spend it.'

'I think not,' said Charles, still speaking in the

calmest tones. 'You had better let me go. I cannot work with you as another man could.'

'Why not? Because you were once my master? That's nonsense! You may be a little sore just now, but that will soon leave you. I foresee that we shall get on very well together.'

'That is impossible!'

'Don't say that. You will find that I treat you well, and, if we can't be warm friends—though I don't see why we shouldn't—at least we shall be on good terms together.'

'That is impossible! You must know it as well as I do. You had better let me go.'

Dick laughed.

'Why are you so obstinate?' he said. 'Really, you will oblige me to say that I cannot afford to part with you.'

'Cannot!'

'That's it. I have resolved upon having you as my partner—you ought to consider that as a very flattering compliment—and I can't let you slip out of my hands just now.'

'You had better let me go.'

Dick laughed heartily.

'Well, you are the queerest fellow I ever met

with! I show you that it is for your good to stop with me, and you won't see it. You don't expect me surely to say the same thing half a dozen times over.'

Charles rose from his seat, and stood with his hand resting on the back of the chair.

'For the last time I warn you, you had better let me go.'

'And I repeat that I can't afford to part with you.'

'Very good!'

With these last words, uttered in a low, subdued tone, Charles left the room.

It would have been unnatural in Dick if he had not perceived the state of Charles's mind. He understood the menace contained in the latter's words, and yet he was very little affected by them. He believed that the hidden threat would not be carried out, and he cared as little as most men for the vain blusterings of others.

But, as time went on, and Charles's sullen humour showed itself more and more plainly, Dick began to understand the perilous position in which he stood. He foresaw that the time might come when Charles's passions would get the upper hand,

and when it would depend entirely upon his own watchfulness whether he survived it or not. And this time was always potentially near, for a quarrel might spring up at any moment by the chance utterance of a few antagonistic words.

There was an easy way of releasing himself from this unpleasant position, yet Dick declined for an instant to consider it. He had said that he would not allow Charles to leave him, and he determined resolutely to abide by his word. He was no coward, and he believed himself quite a match for Charles in a fair fight; for, whatever faults the latter might have, he did not consider him capable of resorting to underhand means to satisfy his vengeance. There would probably be a sudden explosion of temper on his part, and he would then make an open attack upon the object of his hatred.

To be ready for any outbreak of this nature, Dick bought a handy little revolver, which could be carried with ease in the breast-pocket of his coat. Thus armed, any anxiety he might have felt for his own safety quickly subsided, and he was prepared to carry on his intercourse with Charles in his usual calm, unswerving manner.

In this condition matters remained for some time,

Dick continuing to adopt towards his companion the free and familiar behaviour of a kindred spirit, and Charles sullenly submitting to his degrading situation. This period of quiet had the effect of lulling to a great extent the suspicions in Dick's mind that his associate was still meditating a severance of their connection, and he was beginning to hope that time was opening Charles's eyes to the folly of his conduct, when a strange move on the latter's part undeceived him.

He had asked Charles to present, as usual, a cheque at a certain bank to provide cash for their mutual wants, and had met with an unexpected answer.

' Suppose I decline ?' said Charles frowningly.

' But you won't,' replied Dick, with a confident smile.

' Why not ?'

' Why not ? Why, because you don't like going about with empty pockets, which you'll have to do if you don't cash this cheque.'

' Very well. I'll try empty pockets.'

' Now, now, my good fellow, don't be absurd. You know you can't do without money. Here, take the cheque, and be off.'

He held out the cheque, but Charles made no movement.

'I have already declined,' he said.

'Pshaw! what nonsense this is! Have you forgotten your sweet little friend, Miss Topsie? What will she say, do you think, when you visit her, and, in answer to her coaxing, show her your empty pockets? Will she be very eager to see you? Will she be as loving as ever?'

He imagined he saw signs of hesitation on Charles's face, and he proceeded in a persuasive manner:

'Come, come! You didn't mean what you said, I'm sure. You forgot little Topsie. Here, take it.'

Charles was silent for a few moments; then he said, in a harsh voice:

'I tell you again, I decline. Don't press me any more.'

'Very well,' said Dick calmly. 'You'll find out your mistake when Miss Topsie casts you off like an old dress. Ha, ha! Won't she be pleased to see you next time you go!'

Charles turned upon him angrily.

'You had better keep your tongue still, unless——'

'Well, what?' asked Dick, as Charles paused. "'Pon my word, your society is almost as cheerful as a Quaker's wedding. Why, a mute at a funeral has ten times more fun in him than you. I advise you seriously, my dear fellow, to try and make your manners a little more agree——'

He broke off suddenly, perceiving a fierce light glowing in Charles's eyes, like the signal of an approaching outburst of rage; and, putting his hand in his breast-pocket, he produced his revolver.

'A neat little weapon, isn't it?' he said. 'I bought it in case I might be suddenly attacked. It's just as well to be prepared. Don't you like the look of it? Well, I'll put it away. Now I must be off to raise a little money, until you have reconsidered about the cheque. Good-day.'

With these words he rose from his seat, and left the room, smiling.

The result of Charles's determination not to accept any further supplies from Dick at the price of having to do the latter's dirty work befell as his astute companion had predicted. Miss Mandeville suddenly became very lukewarm in her affection when she found that he had no longer the means to gratify her costly whims, and considerately told him that she thought it desirable that their friendship should cease. She had found, she said, that her heart no longer beat at his approach—in fact, that it had begun to beat at some one else's approach—and she had given orders that for the future he should not be admitted into her house.

Curiously enough, this passionate admirer of hers received the news of his dismissal as though he had expected it, and had steeled his heart to meet it with fortitude; for he said not a word, but simply turned his back upon her, and went from her presence.

The state of his feelings may well be imagined after this event. His sullenness increased to an almost unbearable degree, and it was noticed with alarm by Dick that he was seeking solace from his overcharged mind in drink. Having nothing now to take him away from Deadmen's Court, he would remain for hours shut up in his bedroom with a brandy bottle by his side, emerging in the evening with bloodshot eyes and trembling limbs.

Dick watched all this with much anxiety. He felt that, though Charles sober might be trusted to act with some degree of caution, Charles under the influence of drink would be a wholly irrational animal, only too capable of yielding blindly to any revengeful impulse engendered by his hate.

It was an awkward position, but Dick was the last man in the world to accept it as irremediable ; and upon such stout-hearted men Dame Fortune has a way of bestowing unexpected aid.

CHAPTER X.

For several days after he had noticed this new tendency on Charles's part, Dick kept his wits busily at work in the hope of hitting upon some plan by which he might either cure Charles of his folly, or ward off any ill effects of it from himself.

He began to lose a little of his composure in constantly dwelling upon the subject, and no longer regarded death as an improbable contingency. This resulted from no diminution of his natural courage, but merely from a diminution of his confidence of being able to arrest the fatal stroke. This feeling grew as day by day passed without any plan following upon the constant exertion of his intellect, and, as has happened to other men in similar circumstances, he became at length impressed with the idea that the grave was already yawning for him. He felt that the hand of Destiny was upon him, and that no exertion on

his part could avert the fate that loomed before
him. He asked himself, Why should I not fly?
and answered himself in the same breath, I know
I shall not fly.

Dick was a thoroughly brave man, and had as
little fear of death as any philosopher who has
settled in his own mind that life is a thankless
gift; but constant brooding on the prospect he
had conjured up in his mind acted by slow and imperceptible degrees on his nerves, and unhinged
them.

There was one point connected with his disagreeable reflections which troubled him much, and
that was that Charles might escape from the consequences of his crime. The solitude of Deadmen's
Court, the unlikelihood of anyone paying him a
visit, the ease with which a dead body might be
concealed, were all favourable to the perpetration of
the crime without risk of discovery. He thought
and thought on this point, to the exclusion of the
more important point of preventing the crime
altogether. Death would be robbed of half its
bitterness, he felt, if, in dying, he could but know
that his murderer would meet with his just re-
quital.

He was one evening strolling listlessly about the streets, with his mind concentrated on this one absorbing thought, when he was accosted by a woman with a baby in her arms, who asked him for aid. He glanced at her, and noted her haggard, careworn features, and the ragged, dirty garments in which she was clad. His own melancholy thoughts made him feel charitably disposed towards her, and he was putting his hand in his pocket to find a coin, when his eyes rested on the baby. He made a movement of surprise, and kept his glance riveted on the child for a few moments, as though some strange idea—barely credible, yet possible—had occurred to him; then he turned to the woman again, and scanned her features intently. The woman, alarmed at his conduct, was about to make a retreat, when her footsteps were suddenly arrested by the sound of two words:

'Omega Hewitson!'

They had proceeded from Dick's mouth. He followed up his first exclamation.

'I know you; you are Omega Hewitson. Don't deny it.' Then, seeing that the woman was terribly agitated, he added, in persuasive tones, 'Don't be alarmed! I will be a friend to you.'

After a pause of a few moments, during which Omega was in her turn endeavouring to arrive at the identity of her new friend, she said :

'I seem to remember you; but it doesn't matter. I am cold and hungry ; so is my baby. Help us !'

Dick led the way to a cookshop lying in one of the back streets ; and, while Omega and her child were swallowing the food with the voraciousness of half-famished animals, he stood silently by, occupied with the new thoughts that this un-expected meeting had suggested to him.

When Omega had satisfied the demands of nature, she took Angharad in her arms, and was preparing to leave the shop, when Dick broke silence.

' Where is your home ?' he asked.

Omega pointed through the open door.

'There !' she replied.

'Come with me,' said Dick. 'I will find you shelter. Don't be afraid of me ; I am your friend.'

Omega followed him docilely, until they were passing by a public-house near the entrance to Deadmen's Court, when she stopped and gazed wistfully at the glaring windows.

' I am so thirsty,' she said apologetically.

Dick humoured her craving, and they passed on.

Entering Deadmen's Court, he paused at the house opposite to that in which he and Charles were living, and, taking a key from his pocket, opened the door. Omega followed him into a room on the first floor—very similar to the one over the way, only almost bare of furniture. There was an old, worn-out sofa in one corner, to which Dick pointed.

'You will have to do with that to-night,' he said. 'To-morrow I will find you something better.'

Omega thanked him, and, weary with walking, went to the sofa, and sat down. Angharad had fallen asleep in her arms. Dick was leaning against the mantelshelf in thought. At last, he turned to Omega.

'How long,' he asked, 'have you been wandering about in search of shelter?'

'For two days and two nights,' she replied. 'I had no money, and my landlady turned me out into the streets. I slept on a doorstep last night; I was nearly dead with cold. You won't turn me out of this place?'

'No, if you are quiet and do as I bid you. I

live opposite; you can see my room. There is a beam of wood that runs across from your window to mine. I will visit you every morning, and see that you want nothing.'

'You are very kind. I seem to remember you.'

'I remember you under very different circumstances—when you lived with your father.'

Omega started from her seat.

'You remember me then? Oh my God! how different! I was a girl then, happy and innocent; now—— Oh, I dare not think of it. Yet you recognised me. Who are you? Stay, I——'

'I was at Pengwern Park with Mr. Charles Venner.'

Omega rushed towards him, and seized his coat fiercely.

'Where is he? Where is he? Tell me, I beseech you! If I could but meet with him! I would kill him! You know where he is? Tell me! Oh, tell me! If I could but meet with him before I die!'

The vehemence of her passion proved too much for her, and she sank sobbing on the floor. Dick, with a smile of satisfaction, raised her, and placed her on the sofa.

'I know he has injured you deeply,' he said, in a low voice, 'and I will help you in your righteous vengeance. I promise you, you shall meet with him.'

'When?'

'Very shortly. I will bring him face to face with you; he shall not escape you, I promise you. One morning, when I come to see you, I will bring him with me; it will be soon, never fear. You will expect me every morning?'

'Yes, every morning.'

'If I should not come'—here Dick paused for a moment, as though there was an unpleasant hidden significance in his words—'if I should not come, you must make search for me in the house over there. Promise me!'

'I promise.'

'Don't forget! Make search all over the house. I will tell you why,' he added, after a short pause. 'Perhaps he may have visited me—you know whom I mean. He may have suspected my purpose of bringing you and him face to face, and—have killed me. Remember I am striving to help you to revenge yourself for the cruel misery he has caused you. Torn from your home where you were loved and honoured——'

'Don't remind me, for God's sake!'

'Very well. Don't forget your promise. If I miss one day in coming to see you, you are to search until you find me—or my body. Good-night. You will see me to-morrow morning, if all is well. Remember I am your friend, and that I have promised to bring your betrayer before you. Good-night.'

He passed out of the room, leaving Omega standing by the sofa with clenched hands, and eyes fiercely bent upon the floor.

Crossing the court, Dick ascended to his own room, with a feeling of ease in his heart that he had been a stranger to for many days. He found Charles seated by the table with a bottle of brandy before him, half empty. His face was flushed and heavy, and wore the sullen expression that had now become habitual to him. Dick walked to the table' and took possession of the bottle.

'You've had quite enough of this, my good fellow,' he said. 'I shan't let you have any more. You and I must have a talk together, and settle matters. You're not quite yourself now; to-morrow will do. Now go and sleep off the effects of your bout.'

Charles left the room without a word, and Dick,

after having carefully locked the door, retired to rest.

On the morrow, he duly visited Omega, and brought her sundry articles to render the room more comfortable. He inquired if she remembered her promise.

'Yes,' she answered. 'I should have gone to look for you if you had not come.'

'I have good news for you,' he said. 'I have seen him.'

'Where ?'

'Not so very far from here. Trust to me to bring him face to face with you. I can say no more now. Is there anything I can do for you ?'

'I want money to buy food.'

'Well, here's half a sovereign; be careful of it. Just fancy you, a lady born, taking money from me, and all through his treachery. I thought you would have been the wife of some great man in the county—well, I'll say no more. You will never forget what you owe to him ? No ! Good-bye. Expect me to-morrow. Good-bye.'

He was leaving the room, when he turned back.

'One day,' he said, in a thoughtful tone, 'I may not come; I shall look to you to keep your promise.

I should not sleep soundly in my grave if he were to escape unpunished. Good-bye. You are my avenger as well as your own!'

With these prophetic words he left the room.

Omega was greatly agitated by the thought that her betrayer was living at so short a distance from her present habitation that Dick could have seen him before paying her his early visit. She passed the morning in a strange, vacillating fashion : one moment standing motionless with eyes half closed in meditation ; the next, engaging with half-frenzied vigour in some domestic work. Towards the end of the afternoon, the persistency of her thoughts and the restlessness of her nerves became so intense that, having attended fully to Angharad's wants, she threw on her bonnet, and rushed rather than walked into the street.

She had in her pocket a considerable part of the half-sovereign which Dick had given her, and, as she passed by each public-house, her hand stole into her pocket, and seized hold of the money with a convulsive grasp. At each successive house, the temptation to enter became more and more irresistible ; her hand closed more tightly upon the money, her throat became more parched, and her steps seemed to draw her more easily towards the half-opened doors. Under such circumstances, the result was inevitable; the feeble will soon surrendered to the overpowering force of the enemy.

There is no limit to the swallowing capacity of a man or woman who has made Drink a master—except the pocket. When that is exhausted, the landlord recognises, in spite of hiccoughing protests, that the limit has been reached, and promptly ejects his customer. He is the brigand of civilization; he first strips his victims, and then sends them forth naked and helpless into the world.

Before evening had well come on, Omega found herself again in the street, without a penny-piece in her pocket, and with whirling head and tottering steps. She essayed to walk forward, quite unconscious of the direction in which she was going, but quickly lost her balance, and fell.

The usual crowd collected, and the usual policeman made his appearance on the scene; and the incident might have furnished no new experience to Omega had she not become violent, and resisted the law. It was the second occasion of her visiting the police-station, and the Inspector, on hearing the constable's account of her fractious conduct, jocularly remarked that a fortnight on prison-diet would no doubt rid her of her stock of superfluous energy.

Thus it happened that, when Dick returned to Deadmen's Court in the evening, the guard he had set to watch over him was missing from her post. Unaware of this important fact, he mounted the stairs gaily, determined to have that explanation with Charles which he had referred to in their brief conversation on the previous evening.

Charles was seated near the table—lighted by a single candle—on which were spread the remnants of a frugal meal.

'Ah! You have dined!' cried Dick cheerily, as he threw aside his hat and overcoat, and sat down. 'Come, that's a good thing, for you can listen to what I've got to say better now that you've something solid inside you.'

Charles kept his gaze riveted on the table, and made no reply.

'What I want to say is shortly this,' continued Dick, moving his chair so that he faced his companion. 'Since you refused me your aid in my— what shall I say ?—my professional concerns, reflection will have shown you how absurd you were in allowing a few sentimental scruples to rob you of the free-and-easy life you are so fond of living. Now I put it to you plainly. Don't you think you had better shake hands with me and acknowledge your mistake, instead of sulking all day in a corner by yourself?'

Charles made no answer, but knit his brows savagely.

'It comes to this, you know,' continued Dick, with a shade of annoyance in his tone, 'that you must choose either to be my friend or not my friend. If the former, then I will share with you fairly whatever gains I make; if the latter, then I shall have to take means to prevent you from doing me and my plans any harm.'

'What are your means?' asked Charles hoarsely.

'You would like me to tell you? Well, I shan't.'

Charles smiled ironically.

'Oh, don't mistake me,' continued Dick, somewhat losing patience. 'I never make threats unless I can carry them out. I know what I can do, and I tell you frankly you will have to swallow your pride, and do as I bid you. You must either assist me voluntarily or compulsorily.'

'You dare to tell me this!' cried Charles fiercely, half rising from his chair.

'Sit down, my good sir,' said Dick coolly, moving his right hand towards the breast-pocket of his coat. 'Remember, I carry a little instrument which has a speedy way of checking any violence. To tell you the truth, I am beginning to lose my regard for you. You have a little too much silly pride about you, and cannot reconcile yourself to circumstances; besides, you're a devilish bad companion with your eternal fits of sullen humour. Still, I have initiated you into my affairs, and can't afford to let you go. You'll have to do as I bid you; and if you are wise, you'll accept the position before I have to employ other means than words.'

During this speech Charles was moving uneasily in his chair, as if only restrained from springing upon his adversary by a knowledge that the latter was armed. At the conclusion, he rose to his feet, and, turning upon Dick a look of the deepest hate, said with forced calmness :

'You will regret your words. I have warned you. You have paid no heed to the warning. So be it !'

'Pshaw !' exclaimed Dick, also rising ; 'you cannot terrify me with your threats. I know you too well.'

'You do not know me!'

'I know that you're a very sharp, cute fellow, who wouldn't risk your neck for nothing.'

'I have sworn in my heart to have revenge, and I shall keep my word!'

'Keep your word?' cried Dick scornfully. 'That's a virtue of yours, is it? May I ask whether you kept your word with Miss Omega Hewitson?'

Charles started back, and the fierce look on his face turned into one of surprise; but it was only momentary, and gave place as Dick proceeded to a hot flush of anger, indicating the terrible passion that was bubbling up within him.

'You don't answer?' continued Dick, with a light laugh. 'Well, perhaps you are right. Suppose I were to tell you that I contemplate bringing you and your old love face to face again? Oh yes; I've renewed my acquaintance with her, only within the last few days. She has come down, I can tell you. She walks the streets in search of a livelihood. She has to thank you for that. She's altered, too. If she had not been quite so old-looking and dirty, possibly I might have offered——'

The sentence was never completed, for Charles,

with a sudden movement, seized a knife from the table, and sprang furiously upon his enemy. The latter, taken at a disadvantage, could do no more than thrust his hand into his breast-pocket and clutch the revolver before the steel was buried deep in his side. The fatal act done, Charles released his hold on the knife, and drew back towards the table, covering his eyes with his hand to blot out the awful scene from his sight. Dick staggered backwards to the window, and leant against it motionless for a few seconds; then, conjuring the old cunning smile to his face, he drew forth the revolver, and pointed it towards Charles. But as he did so, a film came over his eyes, and, raising his hand jerkily to a level with his brow, he attempted to brush away the obscurity. A moment later, the hand holding the revolver fell heavily to his side, his head sank upon his chest, and his body toppled forwards to the ground. He lay there motionless—dead.

Thus vengeance had played its desperate part, and had given birth to that most piteous of nature's outlaws—the murderer.

BOOK VI.

CHAPTER I.

LIFE and death are sometimes separated by so frag-
mentary an interval, that it is difficult to comprehend that the intervening period has actually passed,
and that the pulsating heart and the rest of the
human machinery have stopped for ever. The
careless laugh has hardly yet died out; you hear it
still ringing in your ears—but the laugher is silent
for evermore. It is as if an invisible hand, armed
with a miraculous sword, had descended, and
severed in one swift and unerring blow the tendons
that bound its victim to life. There was a being—
there is a corpse. Silence succeeds noise, and stillness motion. The restless has found rest. Life has
played his noisy part; Death follows in his silent
rôle. Unexpected, perhaps, but ever ready at hand.
It is a pregnant thought that the shadow of death
is ever projected on the living life: one moment's

pause, the imperceptible overshadowing becomes a total eclipse.

Dick, who but a few moments ago was an embodiment of human vigour—full of the spirit of life—was now lying motionless in death. It took Charles many minutes to realize this fact. He drew his hands away from his eyes—after waiting in vain for sounds of life—and glanced towards the body. The head rested, face downwards, upon one arm, while the other, outstretched, still clutched the revolver. He advanced stealthily towards it, half expecting that it would of a sudden rise from the ground and hurl itself upon him. He knelt down by its side, and touched the face with his hand. It was still warm. Could this be Death?

He remained in thought for a short time, pulling at his moustache perplexedly, and gazing abstractedly before him, keeping perfect silence, even to his breathing, so that no sound of it could be heard. Then he placed his two hands beneath the body, and turned it over. The face was visible, and he drew back in alarm at perceiving upon it the peculiar, cunning smile that had always had for him so hateful an appearance. Death had stereotyped it upon the immobile countenance of the dead man. He had smiled as the land of the invisible had opened to him.   Why?   Because he believed he had provided for the hanging of his murderer, and was satisfied.

Charles returned to the side of the corpse, and gazed long upon the upturned face.   The eyes were cold and glassy—the light of the soul had gone from them ; the expression was calm and undisturbed— but for the accursed smile.

Charles gazed upon it with mixed emotions.   He had hated Dick with intensity during the last few months of his life, and the act of vengeance in which this hatred had culminated was too recent to have lost its relish.   In one moment he had satisfied his deep yearning for revenge, and had freed himself from an intolerable thraldom—at the price of becoming a murderer.   He was marked for ever with the brand of Cain ; and that meant to be treated by his fellow-men as a species of wild beast, to be hunted down and killed without mercy.   He knew nothing as yet of the pricks of conscience— that knowledge was to come.

Yet the thought of the consequences to which he had laid himself open quickly trod upon the heels of his crime, and he began slowly to feel that he had committed a foolish act, which might have a

highly disagreeable result. He half regretted that
he had not stomached Dick's insolence as the
picture of the unpleasant end which the law has
prescribed for homicides presented itself to his
mind. He shivered slightly, and felt a wave of
chilliness pass down his back. To be hanged!
What a finish to his career!

This thought naturally led to his considering the
means of avoiding the legal penalty of his crime.
There was no reason why anyone should know of
it. No one in the locality knew either Dick or
himself, and no one would think of venturing inside
the house. Here, he could not help thanking the
lifeless Dick in his heart for having chosen a spot
so well adapted to the safe commission of a bloody
deed. He could afford to proceed with deliberation
in the matter, and thus provide against every
chance of detection. The first thing to do would be
to get rid of the body, and then he could decide
where to betake himself to beyond the reach of the
long arm of the law.

At this stage of his deliberations the solitary
candle suddenly went out, and left him in darkness. This was followed by a neighbouring clock
solemnly chiming the hour of midnight. It was

time to seek rest, to be prepared for the labour of the morrow.

With the darkness came certain uneasy thoughts to Charles. It seemed to him that the pale face of the corpse stood out from the dim background with a ghastly whiteness, and that the eyes—though hidden and unseen—were directed towards him. He combated this foolish fancy, and reassured himself for a time by dragging the body into a darker corner of the room ; but the same phenomena very quickly reappeared. He despised timidity, and would have then and there sought his own bed-room ; but, as he moved towards the door, he was irresistibly drawn back to the corpse. He felt he dared not stir far from it; strange to say, its proximity sustained his courage.

He lay down by its side, and soon dropped into a troubled sleep. He dreamt, not of the crime, but of many little incidents that had happened to Dick and himself during their acquaintance. In all of them there was a strong undercurrent of bitterness that made them unpleasant reminiscences. He saw Dick again in the full vigour of life, and yet somehow the face was never free from that haunting smile of mingled cunning and urbanity

Once, in his dreams, he tossed his right hand about, and it fell upon the cold, pallid face of the dead man. He woke—with a shriek, and in a moment the perspiration was running from him in streams. He could not go to sleep again, but lay back with eyes alternately opening and closing—as though to assure himself that the body was still in its place —until the cold grey light of morning broke into the room. He felt too tired to rise at once, and lay thus until the clock sounded the hour of ten.

He dressed himself quickly, and, with a view to altering his appearance, omitted to shave. He, however, glanced at himself in the glass. His eyes were heavy and black, and there were strange wrinkles round the angles of the mouth and upon the brow. This gave him the appearance of a man some ten years older than himself—the result of one night of watchful anxiety.

He returned to the room in which the body lay; it had a strange fascination for him. The features were pale and rigid, and ghastly from the un-natural smile that was on them. He drew his eyes away, but could not keep them away for long. This strange weakness of will irritated him, and, to aid him in fighting against it, he covered the body with a thick rug which he took from Dick's bed. In covering it, he noticed the revolver, which was still clutched tightly by the dead fingers. He had much difficulty in removing it; but he succeeded by the exertion of great force, and, finding it still loaded in all the chambers, transferred it to his own pocket.

He began to feel hungry, but dared not venture out in the streets in broad daylight. He had an impression that there was something in his look which would tell everyone that he had committed murder. And perhaps, in a degree, he was right; for the face is only the index of the mind.

He felt unequal to the task of hiding the body that day, and resolved to put it off until the morrow. A day or so would not matter; besides, it would give him time to decide upon the best place in which to hide it. Thus, he passed the day in deliberation.

In the evening, when a solemn darkness had invaded the room, bringing with it appropriately gloomy thoughts, Charles put on his hat, and ventured forth into the streets. He was still under the influence of his fear that his face might betray him.

He kept as much as possible away from the glare of the lamps, and bent his head down when anyone went by.   Once, he noticed an old man who seemed to give him a suspicious look as he passed; he flushed to the roots of his hair, and broke into a run.   It was only an idle fancy.

He walked on rapidly, scarcely caring in which direction he went, so long as he avoided the light, and kept in motion.   He passed by a gloomy building, with a blue lamp above the door; it was a police-station.   On the wall he saw posted a placard, and heading it, in large letters, the word

'MURDER.'

He felt rooted to the ground for a few moments; then turned and fled.

At length, he regained his courage sufficiently to stop in front of a small provision-shop.   He paused before entering, and, peeping in at the door, saw the proprietor — a fat, stupid-looking man—immersed in a newspaper.   He entered, and made his purchases..   As he was stowing away the things in his pocket, the proprietor looked up from his newspaper, to which he had zealously returned, and said :

' Terrible murder that, eh ?'

Charles blanched with fear, and stammered :

' What ?'

' Haven't you read about it ? Down in Chelsea
—a woman murdered in her bed. I'm reading it
now; it's awfully exciting. Good-night.'

Charles left the shop with trembling limbs and
sinking heart; these repeated surprises had quite
destroyed his courage. He resolved to return
without delay to Deadmen's Court; solitariness
and gloomy thoughts were preferable to the bustle
and terror of the public streets. When before his
own door, he hesitated to enter. He thought of
the dark, gloomy room upstairs, with the body
lying in a corner, and shuddered. It would be
dreadful to pass another night in company with
this spectral corpse, which was constantly appear-
ing before him in his dreams with that damnable
smile on its face.

While he paused irresolutely, there came a long,
wailing cry upon his ears—as of an infant whose
physical needs have been neglected. He turned
round, and listened. It proceeded from the opposite
house. Charles walked across, and was surprised
to find that the door gave when he pushed it.

The cry now came with greater distinctness upon his ears, and it had a strange, pathetic accent that moved him. It was as if a little soul was lamenting its stay in a world so hard and pitiless!

He groped his way up the stairs, and entered a room as dark and gloomy as his own. He heard no cry now; but, in its place, a peculiar catching of the breath as though the child were striving to stifle its sobs, either from apprehension or expectation of succour. He found a candle on the mantel-piece, and, lighting it, held it towards the corner of the room whence the sounds proceeded. He beheld an old ragged sofa, and upon it a small child wrapped in a shawl. The child's face was turned towards him; the eyes were wide open, and were watching him with a timid gaze. He approached to the side of the sofa, and began imagining the child's history.

'A fatherless child, probably, born in the street; brought here by a careless, drunken mother, and deserted. A true specimen of its kind—thin, pale, dirty, and miserable. A pity that they should be born; life cannot have any joys for them. This child is ravenous, probably. Why should I feed it? Why rescue it from that best of destinies—Death?

Well, I suppose the brat must be fed—and live. Come, then !'

The child had been steadily watching him with its big, staring eyes during this soliloquy, and, on its conclusion, gave vent to a cry of satisfaction as he released it from its wrappings. Charles leaned against the mantelpiece, and watched the child as it greedily devoured the food he set before it.

'You are hungry, my young friend,' he muttered. 'You are anxious to live, at any rate, though for my part I feel I have done you an ill service in rescuing you. You will grow up a ragged, dirty little blackguard, cursing the parents you never heard of for their folly in begetting you, and ending your life as you began it on the streets. Well, you wish to live ? So be it! Consider me as your father *pro tem.* You will be a companion, at any rate, and will help me to forget now and then that d——d thing over the way.'

He shuddered slightly, and turned to look at the windows of the dismal room opposite.

'I will stay here to-night,' he muttered ; 'I dare not go back there by myself.'

He turned to the child, who had finished eating, and was watching him with contented look.

'You have finished, eh ?   Well, I'll wrap you up again, and you can go to sleep.   There !   'Pon my word, I think I've done a foolish thing in coming to your aid.   Well, no matter ; you look happy enough over it.   Now, to sleep !   I shall be near you, so no crying.   Good-night.   Stay !   Can you talk ?'

The child nodded its head, and smiled.

'Well, what's your name ?'

'Angharad.'

Charles caught the name indistinctly.

'Carrie ? Very well.   Now, shut your eyes.   Good-night.'

CHAPTER II.

THE Professor, ever since the cruel mortification he had received at the hands of the publisher, had caused much anxiety to the kindly hearts that ministered unto him. He had become moody and silent, and—strangest sign of all—instead of going to his favourite authors for comfort, he appeared to have completely forgotten their existence. He would sit for hours in his easy-chair, gazing abstractedly at the empty grate, and rubbing his hands together in a meaningless manner. One day Miss Hewitson made an attempt to rouse him from his lethargy. She placed a small table by his chair, and upon it laid his well-bethumbed copy of Epictetus. The bait took, and Miss Hewitson imagined she had found the cure; but the Professor, after turning over its pages listlessly for a few moments, replaced it on the table, and returned to his inactive meditations. Upon this the family held an informal council, at which Phillips assisted.

'It is useless,' said Miss Hewitson emphatically, 'shutting our eyes to the fact that my brother is in a very serious state of health. Something, it is evident, must be done at once.'

'It is very painful to see him,' said Mrs. Mappertree, in her gloomiest tones, 'and I cannot think what can have caused this change in him. I have noticed, too, that his appetite is not so good as it was, though the rump-steak to-day was certainly tough and very dear at one-and-twopence a pound; and the butchers ought to be ashamed of themselves, but they never are—they don't care how much the public grumble as long as they get their money. I'm sure I often wish——'

'It comes to this!' exclaimed Phillips, in his loud, positive tones, unceremoniously interrupting Mrs. Mappertree's discursive remarks. 'The Professor is certainly not himself—whether or not on account of the treatment he received from that scoundrel of a publisher doesn't matter—and we want to cure him. What are we to do?'

Having thus shown his legal acumen in narrowing down the issue to be debated, Phillips threw himself back in his chair, and waited for an answer to his question.

'Can't you suggest something, aunt?' inquired Alpha, breaking an uncomfortable silence that had succeeded Phillips's words.

'If I had my way,' said Miss Hewitson, sternly gazing through the window at a tailless sparrow which was twittering on a stunted tree without— 'if I had my way, I would make him lay up for a week or two, and diet him well with beef-tea and milk-puddings. If that wouldn't set him right, then nothing could?'

'As for milk-puddings,' said Mrs. Mappertree, with an accent on the last word, as though there were something tragic in the very sound, 'I think nothing could be better, if you could only be sure of pure milk—and you know how dishonest all milkmen are with the wishy-washy stuff they pretend is milk. Poor Mappertree loved milk-puddings, but then we had an Alderney cow, with a white spot on its tail, called Lucy, which gave ten quarts of milk a day—beautiful milk, as rich as cream ; and I used to watch the girl milking it from the top of a wall, and she knew me as well as possible,

and would come and rub her nose against my hand
in the most gentle——'

'The fact is,' said Phillips, again drowning Mrs.
Mappertree's plaintive murmurings in his deep and
rather gruff bass voice, and speaking like one who
is endeavouring to keep the minds of others from
straying to irrelevant topics—'the fact is that the
Professor is regularly down in his spirits. Just
remember that, and then you'll see the folly of
suggesting milk-puddings and such stuff as a cure!'

Having delivered this reproof, which was accepted
by Miss Hewitson with submission as coming from
him, Phillips jerked himself back in his chair,
and gazed upon the others with a look of true
judicial severity.

'I shall not attempt to enforce my opinion,' remarked Miss Hewitson, regarding the sparrow
through the window with a gentle, if somewhat
pained, expression, 'though I have a strong faith in
milk-puddings as a nutritious article of diet in a
sick-room. But still I may be wrong, and I am
willing to be guided by so sensible a man as Mr.
Phillips. What does he say?'

'Yes, Mr. Phillips,' exclaimed Alpha. 'Please
give us your opinion.'

'I am sure,' observed Mrs. Mappertree, 'we are all quite willing to be guided by Mr. Phillips, though at the same time there are things—such as milk-puddings—which a woman must know more about than a man, though, as I think I said just now, a very great deal depends upon the quality of the——'

'It seems to me,' said Phillips, again remorse-lessly interrupting the flow of Mrs. Mappertree's words, 'if you want my opinion, that there is only one course for us to take—to send for a doctor!'

'But it would make my brother so nervous——'

'Not at all! Let him know nothing about it, and introduce the doctor as a friend of mine who wishes to make his acquaintance. He can then examine your brother thoroughly, without rousing his suspicions.'

'Capital!' cried Miss Hewitson. 'The very thing! We are obliged to you, Mr. Phillips.'

Phillips leaned back in his chair with the air of a man who has received expected homage, and, pulling his pipe from his pocket, began filling it preparatory to journeying down to Westminster.

'I will arrange the matter with my own doctor,' he said, as he pressed the tobacco into the pipe.

'He shall see your brother within the next two or three days, and then we shall know what to do with him.   Tell him, if he inquires after me, that I'm down at Westminster on a very important case, but I'll look in again this evening.'

He rose from his chair, and, bowing awkwardly in the direction of the three ladies, walked out of the room.

In due course the doctor was presented to the Professor.   It was lunch-time, and the Professor had been summoned from one of his strange fits of reverie to partake of the mid-day meal.   He entered the room with a dreamy subdued look, and sat down quietly at the bottom of the table.

'Brother!' exclaimed Miss Hewitson, 'here is a stranger who wishes to make your acquaintance.'

The Professor looked up with an air of surprise, and rose hastily from his seat.

'Dr. Maddison is an old friend of mine,' said Phillips, after a formal introduction, 'and, having heard me speak of you, expressed a strong wish to make your acquaintance.   He is, like yourself, of decided literary tastes.'

The Professor bowed, and gravely scanned the doctor's appearance.   He was a short, stout, middle-

aged man, with a very large round face of a florid
hue, from which no indication of brilliancy of mind
proceeded.   There was, however, a keenness about
his glance and a decidedness about his mouth which
proclaimed him a man who had gone through the
world with his eyes open, carefully noting the
peculiarities of the fellow-creatures he met in his
way.

During luncheon the doctor spoke very little to
the Professor, though his eyes were seldom off him.
This action, which would have disconcerted most
men, passed unnoticed by the Professor.   Indeed,
the latter had completely forgotten the presence of
the doctor, and was eating his meal as though the
hum of conversation about him did not reach his ears.

When he had finished, the Professor rose from
his seat, and stood for a moment as if uncertain
what he should do.   Phillips turned to the doctor,
and nodded energetically to him; and the latter,
following out a prearranged plan, cleared his throat
with a prodigious ‘ Hem !’ and addressed his vacant-
minded host as follows :

‘Literature, sir,’ he said, in a voice of thunder,
which made the Professor look at him in surprise
that so large a volume of sound should proceed

from so small a body—'Literature, sir, is a charming study!'

'It is indeed,' said the Professor, in a gentle tone, that contrasted strangely with the doctor's. The subject so abruptly introduced seemed to chime in well with his thoughts, for, after a pause, he continued: 'It is an excellent employment for the mind as a means of discipline and improvement. It hardens it and strengthens it as a course of athletics hardens and strengthens the body. It acts upon the disposition, too, by weeding out the natural savageness of man, and implanting in its stead the seeds of humanity and wisdom. You will remember the lines,

'"Dedicisse artes emollit mores, nec sinet esse feros,"

which our friend Ovid makes use of in one of his epistles.'

'To be sure,' exclaimed the doctor emphatically. 'Ah, there's nothing like a study of the Latin authors for a young man.'

'And the Greek,' said the Professor, with sudden earnestness.

'Of course!'

'Ah, doctor,' observed Phillips, who was listening to the conversation with intense interest, 'you have before you a man who has been soused from head to foot for the last forty years in the streams of classic learning.'

'Indeed!' exclaimed the doctor, rising from his chair, and manifesting much surprise. 'This is indeed a pleasure!'

He walked to the Professor, and seized his hand warmly.

'This will be a day to be marked in the calendar of my life with a white stone, sir,' he said. 'I am indeed happy in having met you.'

'You are very kind,' said the Professor, with a faint smile of satisfaction. 'I have indeed, as my friend Phillips says, been a faithful student of the great writers of the past from my youth upwards— perhaps to the prejudice of other things. But you, sir, are doubtless as earnest a student as myself?'

'Hardly, my dear sir, hardly!' answered the doctor, with a modest wave of his hand. 'I have certainly endeavoured to use my leisure hours advantageously, but I cannot claim any uncommon acquaintance with the great lights of old.'

'How about Æschylus, and the rest?' shouted Phillips, in an excited manner.

'Ah! to be sure,' said the doctor, turning from

Phillips to the Professor. 'My friend reminds me that I have devoted some time to the study of the tragic poets of Greece——'

'Indeed!' exclaimed the Professor, with a sudden change of manner from mere attention to warm interest. 'This is new to me. You never told me, Phillips. Well, well—a—suppose we adjourn to my own room?'

'By all means!' exclaimed the doctor.

'We are getting on famously,' whispered Phillips to Miss Hewitson. 'Dr. Maddison plays his part wonderfully.'

The Professor led the way to his study, followed by the doctor and Phillips, and the conversation was speedily resumed.

'I can assure you, sir,' said the Professor, standing on the hearthrug, and addressing the doctor, who was seated in one of the armchairs, 'that I am deeply interested in the announcement my friend Phillips has made. That you, an ardent admirer of the great tragic poets of Greece, should so strongly wish for my acquaintance, is a singular coincidence; for I can truly say that my admiration—nay, enthusiasm—for those extraordinary writers is equal to your own.'

'Hear! hear!' exclaimed Phillips.

'I am glad, sir,' said the doctor, looking very keenly at the Professor, 'to hear your words, though Phillips has gone rather beyond the truth in representing me as a deep student of these writers. Merely superficial, I am afraid, sir.'

'No, no!' exclaimed Phillips excitedly.

'Come, now,' said the Professor, addressing the doctor, as though he was disposed to set down the latter's depreciation of his own scholarship to a very proper sense of modesty. 'Tell me, which is your favourite edition of Æschylus?'

At these words Phillips lifted his brow, and looked anxiously towards the doctor. There was a moment's pause, during which the doctor's features were contracted in thought. Phillips cleared his throat by a nervous 'Hem!' and drew himself into an uncomfortably erect attitude in his chair. To gain time, he turned to the Professor and said:

'A—what did you say?'

The Professor repeated his question in the most terribly distinct manner, and leaned forward with his head slightly turned on one side to lose nothing of the answer. Phillips fumbled nervously with his pipe, which he had taken from his pocket, and, to make the doctor's silence in answering the Professor less apparent, blew his nose loudly. At length the doctor, whose face had been for a few moments clouded in embarrassment, looked up, and said :

'Well—a—I am hardly prepared to say which is my favourite edition.'

'Ah,' said the Professor, smiling, 'I see! You are not to be easily satisfied. Probably, like myself, you like one edition best for one reason, and another for another. Now for a further question. Tell me which is——'

But here—on the verge of another perplexing remark—Phillips interposed.

'Dr. Maddison,' he said, raising his hand to command attention, 'has read all the editions, but isn't contented yet. He wants to read more. I have told him I know of one — still in manuscript, through the idiotcy of a publisher—which is the best of all editions for all reasons. The work of a scholar—of a man whom I know to possess all the finest qualities of humanity—a man far and away above——'

'Hush! hush! my dear Phillips,' said the Professor, looking with affectionate regard at his friend. 'I cannot pretend to be ignorant of the name of the person to whom you refer in such commendatory terms. Whether your praise be just or no, it is not for me to say; but I think Friendship is apt to make us partial in our eulogies. The eye of a friend is not always the best with which to see ourselves. As regards the manuscript——'

The Professor paused, as though he could hardly bring himself to decide upon dragging the ill-starred manuscript from the obscurity in which it had lain since it had been so ignominiously treated by a pert, shallow-minded publisher.

'Sir,' exclaimed the doctor, in a deep, tragic voice, 'I shall never forgive you if you deprive me of what I can only look upon as an intellectual banquet of the most appetizing kind.'

'He couldn't do it,' shouted Phillips, banging his fist down with a thud on the table.

'If I could think,' began the Professor, 'that you really regard it in that light——'

'My dear sir!' exclaimed the doctor pleadingly. 'You cannot doubt it. You will let me read your work?'

'Of course he will!' cried Phillips. 'You will know how to appreciate it, doctor—the work, I say, of the profoundest scholar of the day, and I don't care who knows it!'

Phillips concluded his energetic speech by crossing his arms and looking defiantly in the direction of the Professor, who was placidly rubbing the glasses of his spectacles.

'Well, well,' said the latter, 'I thought I had looked upon it for the last time when I put it away after that disheartening interview. Ah, well! it is folly to recall bitter recollections to the mind. However, as you are so urgent, doctor, I will bring it once more to the light.'

The Professor unlocked a drawer of his desk, and tremblingly produced the manuscript. There was a slight layer of dust upon it, which he wiped away softly with his sleeve, breathing a deep sigh as he performed this reverent action. He then laid it down on the desk, and, putting on his spectacles, proceeded to dip here and there among the pages. The two conspirators were behind him, and exchanged delighted nods to express their complete satisfaction at the success that had attended their plan. Several minutes passed without a word being spoken, for the Professor was so lost in his interesting occupation that he forgot the presence of his friends. At length the doctor, becoming impatient, uttered a stentorian 'Hem!' which caused the Professor to turn round in astonishment.

'Dear me!' he exclaimed, 'I was nearly forgetting—— Ah, you wished to read this poor production of mine. Well, doctor, take it; perhaps you may discover in it some features of merit that may compensate you for the trouble of perusal.'

As he handed the mass of manuscript to the doctor, he added in a pathetic tone:

'You will be careful with it, doctor; it is the fruit of many years' earnest labour. I have an affection for it from long association; being the author, it is full of beauties to me, though others may not be able to discover them. I had hoped to give it to the public before I—— Ah, well! It was an idle dream!'

'Come, my good sir,' said the doctor, 'don't say that! *Nil desperandum*, eh? However, I'm a selfish mortal, I am; and I don't care whether the public see it or not, now that I have an opportunity of reading it. Well, now I must be off, carrying my spoils with me. Come, Phillips; you go my way.'

They left the Professor standing in an irresolute attitude by the desk, and staring vacantly at the open drawer before him. As they passed into the street, the doctor said :

'I think we have succeeded in rousing him up a bit; but the effect, I am afraid, is only transient. The vital powers are very low, and, unless you can rouse them to activity, his life is not worth many years' purchase. How well we cajoled him ! He is a very simple, kind-hearted man ; and I'm blessed if I don't read his book, though it is all Greek to me !'

'A better man never breathed !' cried Phillips, who was Quixotic in his friendship; 'nor a braver, nor a cleverer ! I should miss him, doctor, I can assure you !'

'Well, then, set yourself to keep him alive. He has a daughter—you have told me the story. Find her out by any means, and bring her to his arms again.'

CHAPTER III.

A MAN, however great a rascal he may be, has always a tender spot in his heart for little children. It is so natural, that it is scarcely necessary to try to discover a reason for it. Perhaps it may proceed from the appealing force that weakness always has upon strong natures; perhaps from a sense of immeasurable superiority; perhaps from that inborn spirit of humanity which occasionally raises a feeble mortal into a god! Whatever the reason, tenderness towards children, like love towards women, is part of every man's nature.

Thus it was with Charles as regards Angharad. The man, murderer though he was, had still the instinct of humanity within him as strong as ever, and he felt kindly disposed towards the poor, helpless infant, abandoned by its parents to the cold bosom of the world.

There was something also besides mere pity that

attracted him towards the lonely babe. He felt a
certain sense of comfort—of rest from the disquieting
fancies that haunted his mind—in having this child
for a companion. He could forget in her society
the horrible thing over the way, whose image as it
lay in death—pallid and rigid, but with that accursed smile ever sitting upon the lips—had been
indelibly imprinted upon his memory. This sense
of companionship, indeed, developed in a few days
into a more extended and somewhat grotesque
shape. By some self-satisfying process of thought,
he came to regard this weak, helpless being in the
light of an accomplice in his crime—an accomplice
in so far that it might have witnessed the act, and
might have raised an alarm, two possibilities of the
most unlikely character. There was thus established
a tie which bound them together, and which made
it a point of honour that he, as the stronger, should
provide for the wants of his tiny comrade. This
strange idea also expressed itself in his uttered
thoughts in connection with the crime and its consequences, so that, instead of speaking for himself
only, he spoke for himself and the child.

Angharad, on her side, proved that her rough
training in the world, limited in time though it

was, had taught her the value of trying to make favourable impressions on all strangers with whom she might come in contact. Kindness, she had already learnt in the space of a brief lifetime of eighteen months, is a commodity so rarely met with, that, when offered, it should be seized with the utmost eagerness. She was a young lady of precocious ideas, and had already learnt the excellent moral lesson that the buttered side of bread is more palatable than the unbuttered. Such being the case, it will be easily understood that she put forth all her feminine charms to win her protector's heart. She exhibited, indeed, all the characteristics of the most accomplished flirt—a course of conduct in a young lady of her tender years that can only be described as shocking. She had fine eyes—the young rogue knew it—and she played them in the most adroit style on Charles; while her smile was the most winning in the world. Not satisfied with the effect of her glance and her smile—though Charles noticed both, and remarked their saucy sweetness—this young lady went to the extreme limits of a maiden's persuasiveness, and actually— offered to kiss him. This forward proceeding met with no return; but, far from being discouraged, the artful young damsel took to blowing kisses at him from the tips of a chubby little hand, and expressed in various ways her appreciation of his past kindness, and her desire that he should continue to provide for her wants.

Thus, then, these two strangely contrasted beings —the man with the stain of blood upon him, and the child still with the innocent heart of helpless infancy—passed many days together in close companionship, and with a constantly growing feeling of mutual affection. The man recognised in the child a source of relief from the oppressive burden of his thoughts; the child recognised in the man a sustainer and a protector. Their hearts went out to each other; the subtle essence of affection passed from each into each, and drew them together by a tie of steel.

The days passed, and Charles made no attempt to quit this spot. It had become a haven of refuge to him, and he clung to it, without heeding his danger in remaining within so short a distance from the scene of his crime. He felt like a man who has passed through the perils of shipwreck, and has found a friendly spar which bears him safely over the tossing waves, and which he is disinclined to

leave, even for the safer protection offered by the
rescuer's boat.   It had given him peace, and he
knew not whether he should find it elsewhere.
He was content to remain under its sheltering roof,
though the danger of his position might thereby be
increased.

He had never ventured again into his old habitation, and shrank with horror at the bare idea of
passing within its gloomy door.   In his moments of
recollection he beheld as vividly as ever the cold
and rigid form still lying upon the floor, and the face
still wearing that ever-haunting smile.   To see it
in the flesh once more ?   No, he could not—he
dared not !   Let it moulder away under the decay-
ing hand of Death, like the body of the slain soldier
that finds an exposed grave on the few paces of
ground it covers.

As the days went by without anything happening
to break this acceptable monotony, so the danger of
discovery seemed to Charles to lessen.   His mind
grew freer, and his spirits brightened, and he came
to regard his crime with a certain sense of calmness
—even satisfaction—vastly different from the horrible feeling of dread that the mere thought of it
had at first awakened.   Time is equally soothing

to the conscience-stricken murderer and the dejected, discarded lover.

One evening, some three weeks after the commission of the crime, Charles was seated with Angharad in their small room. He had just finished his meal, and was leaning back in his chair watching his little companion. Angharad was toying with a crust of bread on the sofa, and was uttering from time to time those sing-song sounds which denote that the infantile stomach is stretched to its utmost limit. Presently Charles rose from his seat, and, walking to the sofa, sat down by Angharad's side. He placed his hand upon her shoulder and patted it, an action which the child repaid by one of her bright smiles. Charles smiled in return, and began addressing her in gentle tones.

'Well, Carrie, how do you feel now, eh? By Jove, you can stow away a tidy lot for such an insignificant little creature! I'm blessed if you can't!'

Angharad accepted his words as a compliment, and smiled gratefully.

'Yes, there's no mistake about it; you've a fine, improving appetite, and I'd rather keep you a week than a month. 'Pon my soul, I would! Who the

deuce do you think would care to have you on his
hands for any length of time, with such a confoundedly consumptive inside as yours?   And you
have hardly got a rag to your back!   How are you
going to get your living when you and I part company?   Because you can't be so foolish as to think
that I'm going to saddle myself for long with a
dirty, ragged, gluttonous little monkey like you!'

Angharad crowed, and blew him a kiss to express
her delight at his words.

'Perhaps you think I don't mean what I say?
Well, I suppose I'm bound to look after you for a
time; but mind you, you must moderate that
appetite of yours.   Why the deuce didn't your
parents do their duty, instead of shoving it on my
shoulders?   It's my belief, Carrie, that your mother
was no better than she should be, and that your
father was an area thief, or some sneaking blackguard of that kind.'

This amusing description of her parents provoked
a hearty ringing laugh from Angharad.   Charles
moved in alarm, and placed his hand before her
mouth.

'I say, don't make that noise!   You don't know
who's about.   They mustn't catch us, if we can

help it. In a few more days we shall be safe, even
though they find the——'

He gave a slight shudder, and, rising from the
sofa, paced the room.

'What made me think of this now ? I thought
I had done with these cursed thoughts ! What
have I to fear ? In a short time all evidence will
have disappeared—will have disappeared.'

He had approached the window, and was gazing
into the darkness beyond it with a troubled look,
when he gave a sudden start, and staggered back.

'God ! there's a light—there's a light over there !'

He passed his hand over his forehead.

'What a fool I am ! It's only the reflection of
the light from this room.'

He gave a sigh of relief, and sank down upon a
chair, facing the child.

'You are surprised at me, Carrie ; so am I
myself. For the moment I lost my courage ; something came over me which I couldn't resist. I was
foolish, I know. It shan't occur again. In this
lapse of time I ought to be able to look the thing
fairly in the face without quivering like a maniac.
My nerves are unsteady even now; look how my
hand shakes ! You are laughing at me ; you are

right. I am a fool! The thing is done, and can't
be undone—and I don't wish that it could be! He
deserved it! I warned him, but he would take no
warning. He brought me down to the position of
his dupe and tool, and I killed him, and I am glad
of it. He is lying now there just as he fell—let
him rot in peace! Come, let us talk of something
else—something more cheerful. What shall it be
about, eh? Can't you suggest a topic? Mind,
nothing in reference to the—— There I am again.
I can't drive it out of my mind. Listen, and I'll
tell you a story—anything will do.'

He drew his chair close to the sofa, and took one
of Angharad's hands in his own, as if to bring the
idea of companionship more closely before his mind.
The candle was burning low, and the light it cast
only partially lit up the room. No sound but that
of his own voice broke upon the solemn stillness of
the place.

'Once upon a time,' he began, 'there lived a little
girl, whose father and mother didn't care for her at
all, and they wanted very much to get rid of her.
Well, they sent her out one day into the wood—
they lived near a wood, you must understand—to
pick some mushrooms, or toadstools, or something

of that kind, hoping that she would lose her way, and never come back. Well, she wandered about for a long time, until she came to a great lake, on which an old man was rowing a boat. He asked her to get in, which she did, when, all of a sudden, the boat broke in two, and she found herself in the water. Well—you are listening, I hope, for this is going to be a regular good story, though I find it difficult to keep my mind to it—well—— Where was I? Ah, she was in the water. Well, she began sinking—she couldn't swim, and there was no one to save her—and she went gradually down—down—down—— Hark! What's that?'

He raised himself partly from the chair, and bent his ear intently towards the door. In the dead silence there came a noise, as though some one were fumbling at the latch downstairs. At this moment the candle began to flicker, and the room was in semi-darkness, every now and then illumined by a bright flash as the light suddenly shot up. The strange noise continued for several minutes, until at length he heard the sound of the door opening, and of a body falling heavily through the doorway upon the flooring below. There was a long pause, during which Charles remained in his fatiguing position, hearing no sound save the hurried thump of his heart against his ribs. Presently the silence was broken by a stirring below, followed by a heavy, clumsy footstep on the stairs. Slowly the stairs were mounted, with occasional pauses as though the intruder were stopping to gain breath; but at last the ascent was made, and the footsteps were heard just without the door. Charles, with paling cheek and quivering muscles, rose up quickly, and, striding to the door, hastily pulled it open—when what appeared to be a mass of rags and dirt was precipitated into the room. He drew back in alarm, and gazed wonderingly at this strange apparition; then approached it cautiously, and began an examination.

As he leaned over it, a smothered groan caught his ear, and, acting upon this hint, he drew aside some of the covering, and disclosed—a human face. A face discoloured with dirt and bruises, and half concealed by long, straggling locks of hair, which were a sufficient indication of their owner's sex. The eyes were closed, and this led Charles at first to believe that the woman was faint from illness or long privation; but, as he knelt over her, the more clearly to inspect her features, a peculiar aroma conveyed by her breath undeceived him. She was drunk.

Charles was perplexed by two thoughts—Who was she ? and what was he to do with her ? The first he dismissed for the present from his mind, and proceeded to devote his attention to solving the second. He raised the inanimate form into a sitting posture, with its head resting against the side of the sofa, and, having propped it up by placing a chair on each side under the arms, he brought the candle near, and sat down to have a better view of the face.

As he was gazing into it, with a look of mingled curiosity and disgust, Angharad's voice suddenly broke upon the silence, with a word that caused him to start to his feet.

'Mam-my !'

That was all, but it was enough. Charles looked at the child, and saw her smiling affectionately, and holding out her arms towards the uninviting specimen of womanhood before him. He remained silent in astonishment for a few moments; then muttered to himself in a sneering tone :

'So the gentle mother has come back to her babe at last !'

CHAPTER IV.

THE obtrusion of Angharad's mother into his
paradise was an event that could scarcely give
satisfaction to Charles. He was annoyed to think
that his privacy should be disturbed, and his
intimate companionship with Angharad interrupted, in so sudden and unexpected a manner; but
his annoyance was greatly exceeded by his disgust
at discovering in this ragged, dissolute woman the
mother of the little creature whom he had rescued
from starvation and had since come to love.

Now that the child was restored to her rightful
guardian, there seemed to be nothing left for him
to do but to sever his connection with her, and go
forth into the world again to begin a new life
enveloped in mystery and dread. And yet he
was loath to abandon Angharad at once to the sole
protection of a woman who had already conclu-
sively shown her incapacity for protecting her

child. These adverse thoughts, alternating in his mind, occupied him far into the night, and he went to sleep at last without having arrived at any determination.

It was getting towards noon when he was aroused by the sound of Angharad's voice, singing to herself as she lay with her eyes fixed upon the ceiling, waiting patiently for her friend to awake. He rose hastily, with his mind in a blank as to the occurrences of the previous evening, and was giving Angharad the usual morning greeting, when his eyes encountered the form of his visitor prostrate on the floor. She was lying at full length on her back, in a darkened corner of the room, sleeping the heavy sleep that follows a drunken bout. Her bonnet—a poor, faded piece of millinery—had fallen from her head, and exposed the upturned features to view. Charles gazed at them with interest, as far as the dull light permitted, hoping to find some redeeming trait to warrant him in believing that Angharad's mother was not yet thoroughly abandoned. But he could find none, and the more he looked the more he shuddered at the thought of surrendering his tiny comrade to the tender mercies of this degraded woman. He felt he could not do so : he had voluntarily taken upon himself the office of protector; he had lived with the child in close companionship for a period that seemed to him to be reckoned by months rather than by days ; he had come to regard her with strong feelings that were new and welcome to him; and he was prepared to make a heavy personal sacrifice rather than leave her to the cruel experiences that would surely be her portion if delivered over to the sole charge of her wretched mother.   Thus came about a strange transformation—this man, whose life hitherto had been dominated by all the baser impulses of human nature, was learning some of the higher virtues at the mute bidding of a poor, helpless, little child.   The agents to conversion are manifold, and not always conspicuous to the eye of man !

Charles, having thus resolved to continue to extend his protection to the child, felt it his duty to communicate his resolution without delay to the mother.   But though by dint of much shaking he managed to get her for one moment to open her eyes, yet her faculties were still too much under the influence of drink for her to shake off her slumbers.   Charles therefore gave up the attempt to rouse her, and wisely left her to return to consciousness in her own good time.

Angharad being hungry, he next turned his attention to her, and, while she was placidly eating her food, he indulged in a few comments on his visitor, which, though addressed to the child, were in the nature of a soliloquy.

'I am sorry to confess it, Carrie, but I am not prepossessed with your maternal parent. She does not reach the high standard which a woman, having the honour of being your mother, should reach. She lacks some of the more charming qualities of her sex. There is—if I may say so—a want of refinement about her. She is now reposing on the floor—as drunk as an owl! This is not right. This is not what I should expect from a female so closely related to you. I do not think it would be a great misfortune for you if your mother were to cut short her existence in this mortal sphere. That is my earnest opinion. I say it with reluctance, but I think the sooner your parent goes to the devil, the better!'

Angharad smiled sweetly at him, and offered him a bite from her piece of bread.

'Thank you, no; I have some of my own. Now,

the question arises, What are we to do with this confoundedly disappointing parent of yours? We might turn her into the street again, but she would probably come back. There is, to be sure, a short cut through the window, but you would probably object to your relative being dropped from a height on to the stones!'

The idea tickled Angharad, and she laughed outright.

'No, it would not do; she is your mother, after all. We shall have to tolerate her—that's about it. We shall have to take this prodigal mother to our bosom again, and extend our forgiveness to her. We must try to reclaim her. We must break her of her vicious habits if we can. If we can't, we'll give her the slip, and let her go her own way. Under such circumstances, we could dispense with a mother, couldn't we?'

Angharad smiled, and nodded in approbation.

'Well, then, it's settled. We'll give her a chance. If she takes it, very well; if she doesn't, also very well. We are agreed; all right; we will dismiss the subject.'

The day passed slowly by, and still the woman slept, and showed no signs of waking. Charles

10—2

began to be somewhat alarmed at this continued spell of unconsciousness, and was thinking whether another shaking might not be the proper course to take, when, just as the twilight was fading away, she turned restlessly from side to side, opened her eyes, and sat up. Charles sat in silence on the sofa, watching her movements with interest.

She gazed round the room with a dazed, dreamy expression, until she caught sight of Angharad, who was enjoying her first sleep. This seemed to relieve her mind from some fear; for she gave a short grunt of satisfaction, and withdrew her eyes until they rested on her own form. She remained for a few moments motionless, and then, with a sudden inspiration of memory, thrust her hand into the pocket of her dress, and drew forth a large black bottle. She put it to her lips, and drank a long draught; and, having thus satisfied her craving, replaced the bottle, turned on her side, and went off to sleep again.

Charles had made no attempt to intercept the bottle before it reached her mouth; but as soon as she had returned it to her pocket, he approached her and drew it out again. It was a bottle of publican's gin—a kind of nectar that can be warranted to produce the most delirious effects within the shortest space of time. Having placed it beyond the woman's reach, Charles, full of the weariness that comes from inactivity, lay down and went to sleep.

When he awoke in the morning, he was surprised to find that his visitor had shifted her position with the apparent object of regaining possession of her bottle, for it was now reposing quietly within her embrace.

'Come, come,' muttered Charles, 'this will never do! Carrie's mother is not behaving well. We must put an end to this absorbing love for gin. There is but one way to check this sad propensity; we will try it at once!'

With these words he walked to the side of the slumbering woman, and withdrew the bottle from her grasp. It was still about half full—a sufficient quantity of the powerful liquid to poison any person not actually brought up upon it.. Charles opened the window, and held the bottle upside down until it was empty.

'Now, my friend,' he said, as he apostrophised the recumbent body of Angharad's mother, after having thrown the bottle into the silent court, where it fell, shivered into fragments, 'you will have to try and do without your daily dose of drunkenness, or else you will lose your child. I would just as soon that you kept to your habit and drank yourself into an early grave; but, for Carrie's sake, I will make an attempt to reclaim you. In five or six hours you will wake and look about for your bottle, and I shouldn't wonder if your language wasn't nice when you find that it's been thrown to the dogs. Well, I'll put up with it, for the sake of your child, who is still so foolish as to have an affection for you.'

Charles passed the morning very agreeably in the company of Angharad. This young lady, with her usual acuteness, thoroughly recognised the ascendency she had gained over her male companion, and began to assume an imperious manner towards him by no means unusual among the younger members of her sex when they have a man in their toils. She was full of caprices: now wanting to be fondled, and the next moment declining his caresses ; now asking to be set down on the ground, and then demanding to be taken up again. Young tyrant as she was, she made her captive tax his wits in the invention of stories for her entertainment, and as

likely as not fell asleep in the middle of the narra-
tion.   But, between whiles, she favoured him with
abundant proofs of her regard in the shape of smiles
and kisses, and thus cunningly contrived both to
satisfy her own wayward disposition and to keep
alive the fire of his affection.

The mid-day meal having been despatched, and
Angharad having dropped off into the gentle
slumber which in youthful persons of her age
generally follows repletion, Charles sat himself
down in a chair opposite to the still sleeping
woman, and waited patiently for her waking.   He
had leisure to scan her even more carefully than
he had yet been able to do, and, though her face
was partly lying in shadow, he saw it well enough
to give him the impression that it had once been
refined and captivating.   Noticing the grey hairs
intermingling with the black, and the lines round
the socket of the eye and the corner of the mouth,
he thought he could not be far wrong in putting
her age down at forty, though he was well aware
what ravages even a short period of dissipation
will work.

The calculation he had made as to her waking
proved fairly accurate; for she shortly began to

give evidence by her restlessness and mutterings that her lengthy sleep was coming to an end. Charles felt profoundly interested, and watched her movements with eager attention.

Presently she shifted her position, and began to grope about her in search of something. The search being unsuccessful, she slowly opened her eyes and sat up. In this position, her glance naturally fell direct upon Charles, whose face was at that moment wearing a mixed expression—half serious and half playful—as though he were expecting a scene in which the tragic and comic elements would be pretty evenly distributed. He was, however, quite unprepared for the stupendous effect which the mere sight of him had upon the object of his interest. Her eyes suddenly dilated and became fixed; her hands extended themselves with the fingers contracted like the claws of an angry cat; and her breath died away in the uttering of a strange, incoherent sound. But this sudden paralysis of speech and action was over in a moment, and, ere Charles could express his feelings of alarm, she had risen to her feet, and had rushed upon him with a fury that nearly brought them both to the ground.

'It is you! It is you! You devil!' she cried,
in a shrieking voice, while she clutched him with
so fierce a grasp that, sitting as he was, he was
unable for some time to release himself. 'You are
brought face to face with me at last! Look at
your work, you devil! Look! Do you know me?
I am Omega, whom you betrayed! I have longed
for this moment in the hope of vengeance! If I
could but kill you!   O God, why have I but a
woman's strength ?'

The consciousness of her sexual weakness at this
supreme moment, as Charles slowly drew her hands
away from his person and rose to his feet, struck
her with such anguish that she fell upon her
knees, and sobbed as though her heart were breaking. Charles, ghastly in hue, and breathing heavily
from the equally unexpected announcement and
struggle, leant against the wall, and watched his
victim with a strange, half-dazed look.   He had
not an atom of doubt that this wretched woman
before him, whom he had set down in his own
mind as having passed beyond the meridian of
life, was the Omega of old; yet the suddenness
with which the truth had been flashed upon him
for the moment benumbed his understanding.

During this interval he gazed at Omega in a half-conscious manner, seeing her at his feet with her hands covering her face, yet making no sign of comprehension. While in this condition of mind, the sound of Angharad's voice proceeding from the sofa rang upon his ears and restored him to himself. He passed noiselessly by the sobbing woman, and came to the side of the child. Her arms were held out to him, and he lifted her up to a level with his face and kissed her forehead. As he laid her down on the sofa again, he muttered:

'There is good even in evil. You are mine!'

CHAPTER V.

THE one great outburst from Omega on recognising her seducer, though expressed in half a dozen sentences, seemed to have exhausted the whole stock of bitter feeling that had been so long pent up in her bosom, for, when the next morning came, all traces of her terrible agitation had disappeared. Both in face and manner she exhibited a perfect composure, and even greeted Charles in a voice which betrayed no perceptible sign of emotion.

Surprised at this unexpected behaviour, Charles looked at her keenly for a few moments, and then said :

'How is this ?   Have you forgiven me ?'

She avoided his glance, and murmured :

'Yes.'

'What has induced you to do so ?'

'I do not know. Perhaps because you are the father of my child. Perhaps——'

'Never mind; I will take it that I am forgiven. In return, let me say that I regret the part I played, and the misery I have caused you. I have had my troubles too, and they have cleared my mind of its mists. I can see things now in a different spirit, and I am glad to be forgiven. We have our child as a bond between us. Let her bring us more closely together. We cannot repair the past, but we can brighten the future.'

With these words he held out his hand, and she placed hers within it; and a perfect reconciliation seemed to have been effected.

To understand what had brought about this apparent revolution of feeling in Omega, it is necessary to dive into her mind and search out her inmost thoughts. During the past night her mind had been working as it had seldom worked before, all her reflections tending to one point. What was the reason of Charles's presence in this miserable but secluded lodging in Deadmen's Court? That it was due to some powerful cause, she felt certain; otherwise he would never have chosen such a place for his habitation. Had he committed some crime, which required him to go into hiding? This pertinent query brought another figure into her mind.

It was that of the man who had rescued her and
her child from the street and starvation, and had
given them a refuge in this very house.   What was
the connection between him and Charles ?   Her
memory had become almost obliterated by her
recent heavy drinking, but by straining it to the
utmost she recalled indistinctly the circumstances
of the two short visits that Dick had paid her.   He
had talked to her both of himself and Charles ; but
what had he said ?   Bit by bit—with many long
pauses between each as the brain wove the several
broken strands together—the conversations came
back to her mind.

He had told her that he lived in the house opposite—the one connected with hers by the great
blackened beam of wood running from window to
window.   He had spoken of Charles as though they
were in some way associated together, and had
promised to bring him and her—the betrayer and
the betrayed—face to face.   He had dwelt much
upon this promise, and had reminded her constantly
of her wrongs, as though the idea of a meeting
between her and Charles, which would certainly be
anything but agreeable to the latter, was by no
means displeasing to him.   Had he a purpose to

serve in thus arranging for his companion's humiliation—a purpose which might possibly have been
nothing more nor less than to gain an ascendency
over the man who had formerly been his master?
To be sure, he had expressed a fear that his life
was in danger from Charles—and rightly too, if
the latter had suspected him of such a purpose.
The next query in Omega's mind—though easily
springing from the foregoing train of thought—
startled her. Was this man's fear fulfilled? If it
was, then Charles was a murderer—a sufficient
reason for his presence in this secluded lodging in
Deadmen's Court.

Having got so far, her mind naturally began to
start objections to this theory.

The association between Dick and Charles might
very well have been broken off without any such
violent cause as death. They might have quarrelled
and parted, and if—as by some chance words of
Dick's she had felt half inclined to believe—they
had been living together over the way, Charles
might well have removed into his present habitation, intending later, in the event of no renewal of
the connection, to remove to some other locality.
There were several causes which would account for

the fact that Dick had not called to see her. The mere presence of Charles in the house—supposing a quarrel had actually taken place—would prevent his coming; and perhaps, during her absence, he had found out that she was in prison, and had in disgust gone away, leaving the possibility of a meeting between her and her betrayer to chance.

But these objections were not of sufficient weight to make her reject the very plausible theory that had sprung up so naturally in her mind. To enable her to ascertain whether it was the true one or not, she determined to veil her hatred for her seducer under an assumed composure of manner that should indicate her willingness to forget and forgive the past. Once in possession of the knowledge that this theory was correct, she would hold in her hands the means of procuring a revenge worthy of the cruel wrongs that she had been made to suffer. Such was the true cause of the remarkable change of manner that had so surprised Charles.

Whether Charles suspected her purpose or not, it is certain that he abstained with the greatest care from gratifying Omega's desire to learn his secret. In their conversations he always avoided speaking of himself and his doings since he had left his mother's roof, and skilfully turned any observations of hers leading in that direction into some totally unconnected channel.

Thus, on the third day after the recognition, the following conversation took place between them, which may be taken as a type of many others. They had just finished their mid-day meal, and Omega was seated listlessly by the window, while Charles was playing with Angharad on the sofa.

'I should think,' Omega said, 'that you will soon be tired of living in this dull place.'

'Perhaps.'

'Where will you go to then ?'

'I haven't thought about it.'

'You cannot remain here always.'

'Why not ?'

'You would find it so lonely. You have friends——'

'None that I care an atom for.'

'Well—associates.'

Charles eyed her slily.

'In what ?' he asked.

'I don't know,' she replied. 'But you cannot be all alone in London.'

'I am not all alone ; I am with you and Carrie.'

Omega paused for a moment; then began a new attack.

'How strange that you should have been led to the very house in which your child was staying!'

'Why? She was dying—her mother had deserted her. What more natural than that I should have been chosen by Providence to rescue her?'

'You must have been living in the neighbourhood.'

'There is no "must" in the case.'

'But you were.'

'I did not say so.'

There was an interval of silence, then Omega continued:

'You say I deserted the child.'

'Well, it looked very like it when I came here and found her starving.'

'But you see I have come back.'

'Yes.' He added, in a low whisper, 'More's the pity.'

'Ah! You wish I had kept away. You love the child because it is young and fresh; but you cannot love me because I have lost my good looks, and am wrinkled and grey. Who caused me to become what I am—an old woman before my time? Who is responsible for these wrinkles, these grey

hairs ?   Who was it that blasted my life—took me
from happiness and plunged me into despair ? Who
was it ?'

Her eyes were flashing, and her voice was quavering with suppressed rage, when Charles interrupted
her tirade.

'I thought,' he said, 'that you had forgiven me.'

His words brought her to herself.

'It is true,' she said, in a calmer tone. 'I am
foolish to think of the past.   Let us talk of the
future.'

But she was too much discomposed, at least for
the time being, to pursue her investigations, and she
subsided into silence, while Charles continued to
play with Angharad.

Omega watched them in their game with con-
flicting emotions.   She was glad in a way that
Charles should have a fondness for his own flesh
and blood, and yet she could not help a feeling of
jealousy rising within her at the thought that the
child should find a place in his heart from which
she was excluded.   She knew it was hopeless to
expect that the feelings which she had once inspired
within him would ever be revived ; her altered face
and mean condition had made that for ever an im-

possibility. She dwelt again on his muttered wish that she had never come back to step between him and the child, and, watching them as they merrily played together, her heart grew darker, and her desire for revenge more intense.

Striving thus to penetrate his secret, and striving in vain, from the guard which he always placed on his tongue, she had begun to despair of succeeding in her purpose, when one day her mind was startled by the recollection of the promise she had given to Dick—to search for him or his body in the house opposite if he should miss paying her his daily visit. There was the possibility that he might have called upon her on the morning when she had appeared before the magistrate, and, not finding her, have discontinued his visits; but it seemed clear to her that, not having seen him since her return, she was bound to make good her word.

It was no easy matter to find an opportunity to effect this object without exciting the suspicion of her watchful and ever-present companion; but one morning, when the dawn was just breaking, and Charles was buried in deep sleep, Omega slipped noiselessly down the stairs and let herself into the court. She paused a few moments before

venturing to enter the house in which she expected
to find the key to Charles's secret, and shuddered
slightly with a foreboding of the terrible sight that
would meet her eye.   But she was too fixed in her
revengeful purpose to allow any feeling of dread to
master her, and, nerving herself up, she pushed
the door open and walked in with a firm
step.

She found herself in absolute darkness, and again
paused before making a forward step; but her
courage speedily overcame her tremors, and she
groped her way until she reached the foot of the
staircase.   She ascended at once, any fears she
might have felt being lost in the opposing fear that
Charles should wake before she had time to get
back to her own room.   Recognising the similarity
of construction between the two houses, she easily
found the door of the room on the first landing,
and, throwing it open, boldly entered.   But what
was it that made her give a sudden gasp, and sink
back inert upon the doorway ?   Not what she saw,
because the faint light of dawn only showed her an
ordinary furnished room bathed in a cold gloom.
But what was concealed to the sense of sight was
made manifest to the sense of smell.   She fell back

half stifled under the deadly effluvium, and only escaped going off into a swoon by her presence of mind in binding her handkerchief tightly round her nostrils. In the midst of her semi-consciousness, and with her heart scarcely beating under the sensation of horror that lay upon it, she was yet able to feel gratification as the idea of a satisfied vengeance came into her mind. But she was not content without some more demonstrative proof of the truth of her theory, and, strong in her purpose, she shook off her faintness and her fears, and stepped into the room. The light had in the mean-time become clearer, and she was able to see every object distinctly. The only one that attracted her notice was a rug lying in one corner, which covered something that could not be seen, but that raised a conjecture. She approached it stealthily, as though she feared to wake the dead, and lifted one end. A moment later she was flying from the room with a face pale as death and limbs trembling under her, yet with a bright light in her eyes and an eager look upon her face which bespoke the triumphant feeling that stirred her heart.

When she reached her own room she found that Charles was still asleep, and, anxious to recover her composure before he woke, she sat down and began leisurely to try to arrange her ideas.

She had penetrated his secret, and his life lay in her hands—that was the predominant idea that came again and again before her mind, and made her pulse beat with pleasurable excitement. To denounce him to the police, and see him receive the just punishment of his crime through her agency, would be a glorious fulfilment of her revengeful hopes. She had made sure of her theory, and the sooner she brought him to a shameful end the better. She could think of nothing else, and she gradually worked herself up into such a state of impatience that she could scarcely control her desire to rush at once from the house and put the authorities upon his track.

In her excitement she rose from her chair, and went to look upon her victim's face. He was sleeping calmly, with his arm round Angharad's neck. There was a serene look upon his face which told of a peaceful dream, and, as Omega gazed, she saw him draw the child nearer to him as though it was the object of his slumbering thoughts.

This simple act roused her dormant jealousy, and, like a spark that sets light to a carefully laid train of gunpowder, lifted her beyond self-control. Stooping suddenly, she seized hold of Angharad, and tore her from the encircling arm, crying out in a loud violent voice :

'My child shall not lie by his side!   There is blood upon him !'

Charles, starting from his sleep, regained consciousness to hear these terrible words and to see Omega standing before him with eyes darting flames of fire, and with the frightened child held convulsively to her breast.   He turned pale, and a troubled look stole over his face.

'Murderer! murderer?' she shrieked.   'There is blood upon you!   Shall I show you your victim? He is over there, lying dead—with the flesh falling off his bones !   Murderer! murderer?'

The intensity of her emotion overcame her physical strength, and she sank back limp and languid into a chair.   Her eyes closed, and her breathing came in loud, rapid bursts ; while the child gradually slipped from her breast on to the floor.

Charles, who had risen from his recumbent position, sat watching her with a curious expression on his face—an expression at once sad and pathetic.

When Omega showed signs of having recovered her composure, he rose and walked slowly towards her. He stopped within a yard of her, and addressed to her the following words, uttered in a low, gentle tone:

'You have learnt my secret. I admit it. I did kill him, but I had great provocation. I had hoped to escape the consequences of my act, and live a happy life—if it were possible—with my child. No matter! You wish to revenge your wrongs on me—you said so the other day when you recognised me, and I feel that you have the same wish still. Well, you hold the means now, for my life is in your hands. Take it; I will neither make complaint nor offer resistance.'

As he finished, Omega unclosed her eyes, and fixed her gaze upon him. A smile was on her lips, and her eyes sparkled with a triumphant light. He bent his head in silence, and turned slowly away.

CHAPTER VI.

THE doctor's report on the Professor's condition was duly communicated by Phillips to Miss Hewitson, and a family council was called together to take it into consideration.

'I am not at all surprised at the doctor's opinion,' said Miss Hewitson, gazing sternly at Mrs. Mappertree, who had taken the liberty to gape. 'It coincides with my own exactly. My brother is gradually losing his vital power, and, unless something can be done, will go off one of these days without a word of warning.'

'Something must be done!' observed Phillips emphatically.

'That is all very well,' remarked Mrs. Mappertree dolefully, 'but it is not so easy as it seems. When poor Mappertree had his last illness—which he bore like an angel, without uttering a word of complaint, though in his days of health he was greatly addicted to bad language—I could see him fading away every day to the " bourn whence no traveller returns " with a smile on his face, as though he was quite content with his condition, and his last words before he died were " Jane, you have done everything you could for me, and you will meet with your reward in a better world."'

Poor Mrs. Mappertree was greatly affected by this touching reminiscence, and fell into one of her silent weeping fits, which lasted more or less acutely during the whole of the sitting.

'As Mr. Phillips has so justly said, something must be done,' observed Miss Hewitson, after a pause, during which she had been considering whether the religious flavour of the anecdote re-counted by her imbecile friend deprived her of the right to administer a stinging rebuke. 'Something must be done. Well, the doctor has recommended a remedy——'

'And that remedy,' cried Phillips, assuming a severe expression, and crossing his right leg over his left with a fierce movement, 'shall be tried, if possible!'

Miss Hewitson looked down, and meekly echoed his words:

' It shall be tried, if possible.'

Phillips uncrossed his legs, and, rising from his seat, perambulated the room with folded arms. At last, he stopped before Miss Hewitson, and said :

' I am glad to hear you say that.'

Miss Hewitson looked up at him pleadingly.

' You thought I should be against it ? In the past, I admit I have looked with the greatest disfavour at the idea of the return of—of my niece ; but, for my brother's sake, I will help him to seek her out, and receive her back without a word of reproof.'

Phillips perambulated the room again for a few turns, and then resumed his seat and his former attitude.

' That is right !' he said. ' You must subordinate yourself and your wishes to your brother. We cannot afford to lose him. The world would lose one of its brightest lights, and I—a loving comrade. A great scholar and a great friend—is not easily replaced.'

Miss Hewitson sat in silence, and Mrs. Mappertree saw an opportunity of easing herself of her flow of words.

' Ah, it is indeed terrible when the grave has

closed over a loved face, and we feel we are left alone with nothing to do but to nurse our sorrows —and think over the virtues of the departed—and try to forget them if we can, though it is not so easy to do so, for everything reminds us of them. When poor Mappertree died, I nearly cried myself after him, and for weeks touched nothing but a little beef-tea made from the shin of beef, which is certainly the best part to use, and brought myself so low that it is a mercy I recovered, especially with so many things to remind me of him—like his favourite dog, Spot, with a curly tail, which used to bark to such an extent that I had to get rid of it, and the three bantam fowls in an ornamental cage which he had reared from the egg, and had grown up under his eye, which I parted with for next to nothing, and—and—I—I——'

A consciousness that her friend's eye was fixed upon her menacingly caused Mrs. Mappertree to blush profusely, to falter in her speech, and finally to break off in the midst of the relation of her interesting experiences.

'Jane Mappertree!' cried Miss Hewitson, in a tone of eloquent sarcasm, 'I fear you have not sufficient scope here. With such a capacity for exhibiting the depths of imbecility, you ought to mix more with the world. It is not right that you should reserve it all for me. I am not selfish ; you can go when you please !'

'I am sure—I meant nothing,' exclaimed Mrs. Mappertree, in little bursts between her sobs. 'If I offend you—I am very sorry—but I thought—you would like to hear—how poor Mappertree——'

'Tut, tut !' cried Miss Hewitson sharply. 'Be quiet ! I don't want to hear a word ! Mappertree was a brute, and you know it—an idle, drunken brute ?'

'He was very fond of me,' sobbed Mrs. Mappertree, 'in spite of his bad habits, and, when he died, he said to me, " Jane, you have done everything——" '

'There ! We don't want that again !' said Miss Hewitson, knitting her brows and stamping her foot in anger. 'If you are going to keep on snivelling, you'd better go. I am sorry to have had this interruption,' she continued, turning to Phillips, who had taken out his pipe, and was polishing it against his coat-sleeve, 'but I think we have nothing further to say. As I said just now, I am prepared to assist my brother in his search with all my power, and to receive back my niece as though

nothing had happened. You have a great regard for
my brother, I know, and would miss him if he died.
Well, I too should feel very lonely without him.'

The unusual feeling with which she spoke moved
Phillips. He rose from his seat, and, taking her by
the hand, said :

' You are a better woman than I took you for.'

The words, though scarcely complimentary in
themselves, were rendered so complimentary by the
tone in which they were uttered that Miss Hewitson,
in receiving them, blushed with pleasure. She cast
her eyes up to his face in gratitude, and then,
blushing more fiercely, looked down again in agitation. Phillips, stirred by some kindred impulse,
felt the warm blood for the first time in his life
mounting to his cheeks. He let go her hand
abruptly, stood for a few moments looking very
sheepish, and, without further remark, turned and
left the room.

After he had gone, Miss Hewitson fell to musing.
The severe expression that generally sat upon her
features faded away. The wrinkles and lines disappeared ; the eyes lost their fierceness, the lips
their sternness. Her thoughts brought a strangely
calm, peaceful look upon her face, for Phillips's

words—few though they were—had touched that soft spot in her heart which she in common with all women possessed.

While Miss Hewitson was engaged in her soothing reflections, Alpha entered the room, and, without lifting her head, seated herself in silence within a short distance of her aunt. The unnatural pallor of her countenance and the languor of her movements sufficiently attested the state of her health, and the long-drawn sigh she emitted as she sat down equally proved that her condition arose from a mental cause. At her sigh, Miss ¸Hewitson looked towards her, and, by a simple transition, her thoughts were turned from herself to the consideration of that attachment which was evidently the source of her niece's low spirits.

From the date of his departure from Wales, nothing had been heard of Harold, with the exception of a notification that he had obtained a curacy in a crowded East End parish. It was only to be expected that this silence on his part, though perfectly natural after the explanation he had had with her, would press very hardly upon Alpha; and, in fact, it brought her to so low an ebb that she almost began to wish that death would step in and kindly release her from the intolerable burden of her spirits. With true feminine feeling, she kept her sorrows to herself, and grieved in silence over the obstacles that had unexpectedly obstructed the course of her love. Being by nature undemonstrative, her condition had hitherto escaped the quick vision of her aunt; and, had it not been for the deep sigh she had uttered under the impression that she was alone, her aunt might have remained in ignorance until a serious illness had suddenly betrayed her secret.

Without disturbing her, Miss Hewitson quietly left the room, and, with the promptitude which usually characterized her when she had determined upon action, then and there penned and despatched a letter to Harold, begging him to pay the family a visit at the earliest moment, unless he wished to hear that his sweetheart had succumbed to a broken heart.

This letter produced the foreseen effect, for, on the following day, while the family were seated at early dinner, Harold was ushered into the room. The Professor, who was putting a spoonful of rice-pudding into his mouth, nearly choked with surprise, while Alpha flushed slightly, and sank back in her chair, overpowered by the unexpectedness of his appearance.

'My dear Harold,' gasped the Professor, in the intervals of coughing, 'this is an unexpected pleasure. We have not seen you for so long a period that we were really beginning to forget you.'

'Not all of you, I hope,' said Harold, with a glance towards Alpha.

'No, no,' observed the Professor, who suddenly remembered the feeling that existed between his daughter and Harold. 'Of course Alpha has had you constantly in her memory. But sit down. You are well, I hope ?'

'Oh yes,' answered Harold lightly, as he seated himself by Alpha's side.

'Your looks, then, belie your words,' said Miss Hewitson, fixing her keen eye upon him. 'Your face is thin and pale, and more marked than formerly. Which is the cause—study or hard work ?'

'Not study,' he replied, smiling, 'for my time is so occupied——'

'Ah ! then it is hard work !'

'Well, I confess the work is hard, but it is work that I like. You should see the desperate condition

of the poor of my district.   Their houses are mere
pest-houses, and they themselves but white savages.
They dress in rags, have a strong partiality for
drink, and use a language which ladies happily
would not understand.   There's a splendid field for
work ! I would sooner save the soul of one of these
poor degraded wretches than I would direct a
duchess to the road to heaven !'

The warmth of his feelings brought the colour to
his cheeks, and his eyes flashed with inward fire.

'Poor creatures !' exclaimed the Professor, his
eyes absently fixed on the table-cloth ; 'their position is indeed so bitter in this world that they
deserve a brighter portion in the next. Philosophers
have often debated the question whether life be
worth living, but, could they see these poor people
in their squalid homes, their opinion must be that
only the hope of a life hereafter could render such
an earthly life tolerable. It may indeed be safely
predicated——'

But at this point Miss Hewitson, anxious to
leave her pair of lovers to their own sweet society,
interrupted her brother's speculations, and, seizing
him by the arm, led him away from the room,
with Mrs. Mappertree in close attendance.

Left alone, the lovers spent a delicious couple of hours in going minutely over all the trivial occurrences that had happened since their last meeting, and consoling each other for the heart-aches that they had in the meantime severally felt. This conversation proved to be of so restorative a nature, that, when Miss Hewitson re-entered the room with her brother held captive-like on her arm, Alpha had got quite a colour in her cheeks—a change equally noticeable in Harold.

Over the tea, to which Phillips lent the lustre of his appearance, Miss Hewitson, in the most discreet manner, broached the subject of Omega.

'I have determined,' she said, addressing the table at large, but occasionally glancing hurriedly at Phillips to watch his expression as she proceeded in her remarks—'I have determined to aid my brother to the utmost of my power in the prosecution of his search after my niece. If we are successful—as I trust by God's aid we shall be— she shall never have a word of reproach from me. I do this, I need not say, for my brother's sake.'

'Thank you, sister, thank you,' said the Professor, whose eyes were moist with gratitude at his

sister's words.   'You have a true womanly heart—
I was sure of it all along.'

Phillips, with a very serious air, looked at Miss
Hewitson, and, having cleared his throat by a
stentorian grunt, said :

'You have done your duty, ma'am, and I honour
you for it !'

Miss Hewitson coloured with pleasure, and, to
hide her confusion, turned to Harold.

'You will help us, will you not, as far as you
can ?' she said; 'that is to say, in your own
district. My brother and I begin a systematic
search to-morrow.'

Harold readily consented to do as she wished,
and, the tea being finished, retired with Alpha to
a far corner, where they carried on a subdued conversation until it was time for him to go.

'There is a happy future, I am sure, for us,' he
said, as he took leave of her. 'A few years of
disciplinary waiting will only serve to make our
happiness the more complete.'

The excellent effect which his bright, cheery
presence left on the family was seen not only in
the altered spirits of Alpha, but in the zeal with
which Miss Hewitson entered upon the search after

the missing child. With the Professor firmly attached to her side, she passed from one part of London to another, visiting police-stations, hospitals, and homes, but hearing no tidings of Omega. Sternly determined to succeed, if success were possible, she allowed no discouragement to enter her heart, but carried on the search with an energy which seemed never to abate. The Professor, too, fell under the influence of his sister's spirit, and felt the utmost confidence in the final result of their daily wanderings.

'We are rapidly contracting the area of our search,' he would say, when they returned home after a day's fruitless labour. 'It cannot be long now before we find her.'

One afternoon, as they were coming out of a police-station in the Borough, where Miss Hewitson had left behind her the most minute particulars of her niece's person, a woman brushed past them, and demanded to see the inspector. When asked her business, she answered in a loud, excited tone :

'I have come to deliver up a murderer to justice !'

At these ominous words, the Professor and his

sister turned round and gazed with surprise at the new-comer. She was ragged, and dirty, and un-kempt ; and her voice was harsh and unpleasant.

'Come, let us begone from this place,' cried the Professor, in accents of alarm. 'The shadow of crime hangs over it.   Come, sister, come!'

CHAPTER VII.

THE woman who had entered the police-station was Omega. Firm in her purpose to avenge her wrongs, she had lost no time, after listening to Charles's confession, in quitting the house upon her terrible errand.

When she entered the inspector's room, the demon within her was raging as fiercely as ever, and she needed no persuasion to tell her tale in all its hideousness.

'I come to deliver up a murderer to justice,' she said, speaking hurriedly, as though she feared her excitement might take away her voice. 'The murdered man is even now lying where he fell, with the flesh rotting upon his bones. You will send at once to arrest the murderer? I can take you to where he is.'

The inspector looked at her gravely, and said in a tone in perfect contrast with hers :

'Are you quite sure of what you say?'

'Yes, yes; you cannot doubt me. He has committed murder—I swear it! I have seen the murdered man's body—besides, he confessed to me that he had done it. It is true—I assure you, it is true!'

The inspector, whose years had made him cautious in dealing with informers, was puzzled by the eagerness with which she gave her information. To discover her motive, he put a simple question to her.

'Is the man whom you accuse your lover?'

'No!' she replied firmly. Then, in a lower voice, she added, 'He was my lover once, and deceived me basely!'

The inspector lifted his eyebrows expressively, and remained silent for a few moments, tapping the desk idly with his fingers. At length he rose, and, opening the door, called out:

'Sergeant Bateson!'

Steps were immediately heard without, and the sergeant, an unusually stolid-looking young man, entered. The inspector directed his subordinate's attention to Omega.

'You will accompany this person,' he said. 'She

has given information of a murder, and will conduct you to the spot where the body lies, as well as to the place where the murderer is hiding.   You will do this?' he added, turning to Omega.

'Yes, I promise.   Let us go at once; he may escape in my absence.'

The inspector turned again to the sergeant, and spoke to him in a low voice:

'Her story appears to be genuine.   You will know what to do.'

The sergeant nodded in the gravest fashion, and beckoned to Omega to follow him from the room.

Once in the street, Omega led the way—at first almost running in her anxiety to get forward, but gradually slackening her speed—while the sergeant walked impassively by her side, maintaining perfect silence.   In this, from a professional point of view, he was wrong; for he gave Omega the opportunity of dwelling in her mind upon the consequences that would follow the step she had just taken.

She was offering up a human life as a satisfaction for a great wrong which she had suffered in the past.   That was the focus of her thoughts.   The idea of assisting justice—of bringing to light a

horrible crime—was utterly excluded. The dead
man was nothing more to her than a mere item in
the sea of humanity, about whom she felt no
interest. He might or might not have deserved his
fate ; it was a matter of indifference to her. Private
feeling alone had urged her action.

A human life ! After all, was her wrong so great
as to demand such a terrible expiation ? He had
loved her once, and he had told her that he regretted
the infamous part he had played towards her.
There was a bond, too, between them—a child
whom he loved ; not the less a bond because it was
the fruit of lawless passion. She had felt much
jealousy at seeing him shower endearments upon
the child. But was it not natural, and, in its
way, an indirect tribute to her? If he had ruined
her life, his, possibly by the hand of an avenging
fate, had been ruined also. Then why seek to sup-
plement an already sufficient punishment?

A human life ! The life of a man who had once
loved her, who was the father of her child ! What
had she done in her blind rage ? How was it that
her eyes had not been opened to the bloodthirsti-
ness of her vindictive feelings until it was too late ?
Too late ? Was it too late ?

She drew her gaze from the ground, and looked about her. The sergeant was walking stolidly a few paces in the rear, with his eyes calmly fixed upon her.

The desire now to save Charles from the fate that hung over him was as intense as her former desire to bring about his death; and, as she walked along, she set her wits to work to conceive a plan that might avert the consequences of her own headstrong act.

A few moments later she came to a sudden stop, and seemed greatly embarrassed. The sergeant came to a stop, too, and addressed her in a mono-syllable.

'Well?'

'Sir,' she said, in a hesitating voice, and casting her eyes on the ground, 'I have done very wrong. The story I told at the police-station is false. There is not a word of truth in it. Pray forgive me for the trouble I have put you to, and let me go.'

The sergeant took a long, solemn look at her, and then said:

'What made you tell such a story?'

'I don't know. I was foolish, or wicked, or both. You will forgive me?'

She looked up at him, but, meeting his glance, hastily looked down again.

'It's no trouble,' said the sergeant, with a little laugh. 'But, tell me, where do you live ?'

'Where do I live ? Very far from here—with my child. She and I live together, quite alone. You will let me go now, will you not ?'

'I think I ought to take you back to the inspector.'

'Oh no, please don't! Not now! my child will be so hungry. I will come again to-morrow, if you wish.'

The sergeant put on a thoughtful expression, and remained silent for some moments. At last he said :

'Are you sure you won't forget ?'

'Oh yes. I will come to-morrow, and beg the inspector's pardon for my folly.'

'Well, I will take your word. You may go.'

'Oh, thank you !'

Omega felt half inclined to seize his hand and kiss it, but refrained, and hurried away with a glad heart. Looking back at the end of the street, she saw the sergeant still standing where she left him, apparently looking in quite a different direction

from hers.   She hurried on towards the court, eager
to get back and tell Charles of the altered state of
her feelings.   On her way she passed a public-house,
and for a moment was seized with a violent wish to
enter its inviting portals ; but, resolutely casting the
idea from her mind, she walked quickly by it.   Panting from her exertions, she pursued her way, unconscious of the bustle of life going on around her, and
was soon within the friendly shelter of the court.
Entering her dwelling, she climbed hastily up the
stairs, and, bursting open the door, found the room
—empty.

This is what had happened in her absence.
When Charles saw her leaving the house, a great
wave of feeling passed over him.   The danger of
his position came before his mind in all its distinctness.   Unless he bestirred himself, he was doomed
to die the meanest of deaths—a fate against which
his pride revolted.   To escape it, two courses were
open to him—to become his own executioner, or to
seek safety in instant flight.

Life, even to the most wretched of men, is sweet
when death looms near; and Charles, though he had
often spoken as though death would have no

terrors for him, was no exception to the rule. He dismissed at once from his mind the idea of suicide, and determined to adopt the alternative course.

Having formed this resolution, he was troubled by another thought. Should he take Angharad with him? At that moment the child was slumbering peacefully upon the sofa, dreaming the sweet dreams of childhood. Charles clearly saw that she would be a terrible encumbrance to him in his passage through life, and that it would be to his interest to free himself of her; yet he found it a difficult task to bring himself to the determination of abandoning this little being who had wrapped herself so closely round his heart. To leave Angharad—who had been the one bright ray that shone out of a clouded existence, who had roused in him some of the better qualities which mark the reasoning from the unreasoning man? What a hard necessity!

He approached the sofa, and looked upon the face of the child, smiling in her happy dreams. What would be her fate if left to the care of a wretched, drunken mother, who had lost all maternal feeling? And yet, for his present safety and his future peace, he felt it to be imperative that he should separate from her.

He stooped to kiss the tiny lips below him as a parting farewell, and in doing so woke the child, who threw her arms around his neck. A tear stole from his eyes—the first that he could remember to have shed—and, raising her from the sofa, he strained her to his breast.

'I cannot give you up!' he murmured. 'You are my life!'

Bearing the child with him—a shapeless bundle in his arms—he passed down the stairs into the court. But here he came to a sudden stop. A strange feeling entered his system, that began with a desire, and ended in an uncontrollable impulse. He felt impelled by some inward force to visit the scene of his crime, and take a last look at the face of his murdered companion. He had no power to resist, for his feet led him without consulting his will.

Still bearing the child, he entered the fated dwelling, and, swiftly mounting the stairs, burst through the door of the room where lay the corpse. The stifling odour at once seized hold of him, and, reeling across the floor, he had just strength to throw open the window before he sank down in a semi-conscious state. In this position he remained, unheeding the flight of time, yet feeling his weakness, and clasping the hand of Angharad as a sort of talisman against greater helplessness.

When Omega had recovered from her surprise on discovering that the room was empty, she began to speculate on what had happened during her absence. Had Charles, watching her depart, been suddenly seized with fear at the thought of death, and taken refuge in flight?

This seemed the only possible conclusion, and it was to some extent verified by the absence of the child, whom he would scarcely have taken with him had he intended to return. Omega, in the present state of her feelings, was sorely troubled by this thought; and tender memories of the past, when she was still under the intoxication of a first love, crowded swiftly into her mind, and reopened the dried founts of her eyes. She walked to and fro about the room, wringing her hands and looking around her eagerly, in the hope that she might find some evidence to disprove her supposition. There was none, and she was gradually succumbing to a feeling of utter despair, when the sound of Ang-harad's voice, singing a simple, childish song, came through the open windows of the room.

Omega started up to her feet, and stood statue-like, straining her ears to discover from what quarter the sound came. As she listened, her head gradually described a semicircle until her eye fell upon the open window opposite. In an instant her mind had comprehended the situation.

In the excess of her joy she leaned out of her window to call playfully to the child; but, in the act of calling, a terrible expression of fright settled on her face, and her voice dropped into an inarti-culate sound. Her eyes had encountered a figure in blue standing rigidly and silently on the pave-ment below.

Quickly recovering herself, she drew back into her room, and, with beating heart and throbbing temples, set her brains again to work. Was it pos-sible still to save him? There was a chance — slight, indeed, yet not hopeless—if she could warn him of his danger. How was she to do this? Inspiration came to her aid, and pointed out the means. She seized a piece of paper, and pencilled the following words upon it:

'The police are after you. Fly at once if you wish to escape.

' OMEGA.'

As she was signing her name, the door below opened, and heavy footsteps sounded on the stairs. Looking round her in desperation, she espied an old, dried-up ink-bottle, into which she hastily crammed her brief words of warning. Rushing with this to the window, she hurled it with accurate aim across the court. A moment later, the door turned on its hinges, and the sergeant entered.

He smiled blandly as he noticed her position, and walked slowly towards her.

'I am sorry to intrude,' he said, watching her confusion with evident relish ; 'but you will pardon me, I am sure. You are astonished, perhaps, to see me. Well, I must confess I have played you a little trick, for which I also ask your pardon.'

He paused for a moment to look about him, and then said :

'So this is where the murderer lives ?'

'He has fled,' answered Omega shortly.

'But not far !'

The sergeant uttered these last words in such a

peculiar tone that Omega could not help lifting her eyes to his face. He was looking calmly at the open window opposite, from which a pale, haggard face was peering.

The sergeant smiled significantly at the start of surprise which Omega was unable to suppress, and, without another word, left the room.

Omega heard him descend the stairs and issue into the court, the regular beat of his heavy foot-steps ringing with terrible emphasis upon her ears. With a deadened feeling at her heart, which by its utter hopelessness produced in her an artificial calm, she stationed herself by the window to watch the ending of the drama which her own act had ori-ginated.

As soon as the sergeant reached the pavement he gave a subdued whistle, and was joined by a police-man who appeared from the entrance of the court. The new-comer received a whispered command from the sergeant, accompanied by a glance at the great beam of wood over their heads, and ascended at once into Omega's room, where, without condescend-ing to notice her, he placed himself in a position from which he could see all that passed over the way.

The sergeant proceeded leisurely to enter the murderer's hiding-place, and the loud beat of his footsteps could be plainly heard as he mounted the stairs. A minute later the window was thrown up to its full extent, and Charles, clutching Angharad to his breast with one hand and in the other grasping his revolver, stepped bareheaded on to the great blackened beam. His face was deadly pale, and twitched with nervous excitement. His fear had been communicated to the child, whose two arms were pressed tightly round his neck, thus hindering his movements. With no clearly formed resolve, except a prompting to return the child to her mother's arms before meeting his own fate, he advanced slowly across the beam, but stopped midway on perceiving the erect figure by Omega's side. He turned, only to see the sergeant standing at the window from which he had issued.

He paused, and, letting his head fall on his breast, drew a long sigh of pain.

The sergeant spoke.

'You had better surrender. We are two to one. It is folly to think of resisting us.'

There was no reply. Charles remained motionless, with his eyes bent towards the child, and his

lips moving as though he were breathing some parting prayer.   The nervous twitching had ceased, and
a perfect calmness reigned on his face.

At a preconcerted signal from the sergeant, the
two servants of Justice mounted on to their respec-
tive ends of the beam, and moved cautiously
towards their victim.   Not until they were close
upon him did he appear to notice their presence,
and even then he made no attempt to use his
weapon, only straining the child more closely to
his breast.

The sergeant stretched forth one hand, and the
policeman another, and they laid them softly upon
him.   Then, at last, he seemed to recognise his position, for he suddenly shook himself free from their
grasp, and threatened the sergeant with his revolver.
To save his officer the policeman seized hold of the
arm encircling Angharad, and, in the violent wrench
he gave, caused the child to lose her hold.   She
dropped on the beam and rested there for a moment ;
but, before a hand could be lowered to save her, fell
heavily from it on to the stones below.   A terrible
cry burst from Charles, and with a quick movement
he turned the revolver towards his own breast.
There was a flash, a cloud of smoke, and a dull thud

as his body fell beside that of the little being who had sown the first seeds of a higher and purer life in his fierce, passion-swept heart.

When the two policemen met below, they found a woman uttering piercing cries of anguish over the two bodies. The man's was quite dead, but the child's showed some slight signs of life. The latter was carried silently into the house and left under the charge of the lamenting mother, while the former was borne away with all convenient despatch to the police-station.

CHAPTER VIII.

WHEN Omega was left alone with the dying child, the floodgates of her heart were opened, and the tide of her grief swept out in a resistless torrent. Perhaps till then she had never understood the deep meaning of the simple word 'mother.' This child, though born in sin, was still a part of herself—a tiny copy wherein her own self was reflected—and though she had never shown it a mother's affection, yet now, when the supreme moment of parting had come, she discovered suddenly how dear it was to her. Her heart was racked asunder by the thought of past remissness, magnified as it always is when the opportunity for repairing it has slipped away, and the tears rolled in endless succession from her eyes.

It was a chastening grief, for it brought to her mind a long-forgotten sense of the Omnipotent Hand that guides the universe and the creatures upon it; but her rebellion had been too recent to allow her to think of appealing to the Divine Power for help under her distressful circumstances. She had but one thought—to follow her child out of a hard and unkind world, and seek surcease of her sorrows in the quiet solitude of the grave.

She sat by the side of the unconscious child, watching the flow of the fast-ebbing life, until the shadows of evening came and obscured the light of day. More than once she rose from her seat thinking that the last breath had been breathed; but each time she found the spark of light still dimly flickering.

When the blackness of night had gathered round, she lit a candle, and placed it so that its light fell upon the child's pallid face. Thus an hour went by, when the watcher beheld a slight restless movement pass over the body of the little sufferer. It was the final effort of the body to restrain the flight of the soul; but a moment later, with the utterance of a deep sigh, the movement ceased, and the sudden stillness proclaimed that the soul had conquered. The little life, that had tasted even in its brief space so deeply of the world's cup of sorrow, had passed away to seek a gentler treatment at the hands of the Great Judge.

The knowledge that death had at last stepped in between them caused Omega to sink under a fresh paroxysm of grief, during which she pressed her arms round the body that could no longer feel her caresses, and imprinted kisses on the lips that could no longer return them.   In a short time, however, she managed to subdue her feelings, and set herself to perform the last kindly offices for the dead.   Stripping the body of its rags, she washed it tenderly, and dressed it again in clean garments. Then, having laid it out reverently on the bed, and taken a final kiss, she closed the door behind her, and walked out into the night.

At this moment, when she thus left the house with the longing to follow her child firmly impressed upon her mind, she was the subject of a lively conversation at the neighbouring police-station.   In the course of an examination of the dead man's pockets, the sergeant had come upon a crumpled piece of paper, which, upon being smoothed out, he gazed at with a smile.

'There, sir,' he said, as he handed it to the inspector.   'You see she couldn't help warning the fellow after all.'

The inspector put on his glasses, and traced out a few roughly scribbled words on the paper. They were these:

'The police are after you. Fly at once if you wish to escape.

'OMEGA.'

As he read the signature, he looked up quickly.

'Omega!' he said; 'that's the very woman we've been on the look-out for! We mustn't lose sight of her. Sergeant, you must step round to her lodgings—stay! I shall want you to take the news to her family. Let Williams go and bring her here. She will be slipping through our fingers if we don't keep a sharp eye on her. You may as well start at once.'

In five minutes, the sergeant and Williams parted on the steps of the police-station, the constable walking off in the direction of Deadmen's Court, while the sergeant made his way towards the Professor's humble lodgings in Danes Inn.

The sergeant stepped out at a good round pace, and was soon at his destination. He found the Professor and the rest of the family just finishing their evening meal. His entrance caused some

alarm, especially to Mrs. Mappertree, who uttered
a heart-rending cry under the impression that she
was about to be dragged off to prison for some un-
known crime. Phillips, who was present, quickly
pacified her, and, taking the lead, as indeed his
decisive character entitled him to do, sternly demanded of the sergeant the meaning of his in-
trusion.

The sergeant replied with becoming brevity.

'A young woman has been found, with the
Christian name of Omega——'

'It is my child!' cried the Professor, jumping
up from his seat, with every nerve quivering from
excitement. 'It is my child! My darling child!
She is found at last! Thank God! thank God!'

He sank down again in his chair, and, covering
his face with his hands, breathed a silent thanksgiving to the Almighty for His infinite goodness in
having thus answered his prayers. When he had
finished, he rose up, and, walking to the sergeant,
laid his hand upon his shoulder.

'You will take me to her at once? Yes, of
course. You do not know how blissful your
news is to me. I thank you, from my heart. I
have always loved her so dearly, and—and when

we were parted, I felt as if my heart would break! You have seen her? Ah, is she not beautiful! She used to seat herself on my knee, and lay her sweet head upon my shoulder—— Yes.'

The Professor paused, for his mind had carried him back to a distant past that was full of delicious reminiscences. His hand still remained on the shoulder of the sergeant, who was gazing before him with his most stolid expression of countenance.

Miss Hewitson, with a recollection of the alarming effect which some months back the letter of his unhappy daughter had had upon her brother, was fearful lest the sergeant's abrupt communication should produce similar consequences, and held a hurried conversation with Phillips as to what they should do.

'I am afraid,' she said, 'that it may affect his mind; besides, the shock of meeting with his child will be great. What shall we do?'

'The shock cannot be avoided,' replied Phillips. 'We must be guided by circumstances. You and I will go with him. Get ready at once.'

Then, walking up to the Professor, he touched him gently on the arm.

'Your sister and I are going with you. Are you ready?'

The Professor looked up with a startled air.

'Ready? Ah, yes. Come, my dear friend; every moment's delay keeps me longer from her. My darling child! How I long to fold her in my arms! You have seen her, sir? Is she much changed? Shall I know her again? Know her! I am foolish! I could pick her from a thousand! Those rosy cheeks—those dark, clustering curls—how I remember them! Ah, sister, you are ready. Let us start, then. Come, my dear Phillips. Come, sister.'

The Professor, without further remark, was walking quickly from the room, when he was recalled by Miss Hewitson, who, in a tone of mild admonition, asked him whether he thought it was prudent to venture out at night without a hat or coat. He received this gentle reproof with a light laugh at his own absence of mind, and submitted docilely while his sister pulled his arms through the coat-sleeves, and stuck the hat somewhat fiercely on his head. During the ride to the police-station, he exhibited great restlessness of manner—at one moment talking volubly about his daughter, at another lapsing into a strange fit of silence.   His hand rested upon the window-ledge of the cab, and his sister noticed that it trembled violently.   Placing her own upon it, she drew it gently to her lap—an action that passed unnoticed by her brother.   Phillips was talking in an undertone with the sergeant, and gathering all the particulars known to the latter respecting the poor girl who was the object of their journey.

When they reached the police-station, the Professor's anxiety was so great that he was unable to mount the steps without the assistance of his sister and his friend.

'I am very foolish,' he said, in a tone full of pathos. 'Pray, bear with me. It will be over when I have my child in my arms.'

Meeting the inspector in the passage, the Professor hurriedly put to him the question that was uppermost in his mind.

'My child, sir—she is here, waiting for me?'

The inspector scrutinized his questioner for a moment, and then replied gently :

'She will be here soon.'

'She—she is not here now?'

'I have sent one of my men to bring her here.

He has not come back yet.   You shall see her presently, never fear :'

The Professor thanked him in a low voice, and
joined his sister and Phillips.   He sighed deeply as
he sat down, for he had expected to find his
daughter awaiting him, and his disappointment
was great.   Phillips tried to console him by remarking gruffly that policemen were always so
confoundedly lazy, and Miss Hewitson supple-
mented this statement by observing that they were
shallow-minded as well; but neither remark,
strangely enough, had any brightening effect upon
the Professor's spirits.

The moments glided by, and both Miss Hewitson
and Phillips began to catch some of their companion's restlessness.   They fidgeted in their seats,
and cast anxious glances at each other over the
drooping head of the Professor.   Indeed, the situation had become almost unbearable from the intensity of their feelings, when a constable hastily
entered the station, and held a muttered conversation with the inspector.

The Professor, trembling with forebodings, rose
from his seat, and went towards them.

'Pray tell me your news,' he said, in a broken

voice. 'I fear it is unwelcome; but I can bear it. Do not hide anything from me, I beg of you.'

'You will have to be patient for a little while longer,' said the inspector. 'Your daughter has left her home—don't be afraid; she cannot be far away. We shall find her within an hour or two at most. Comfort yourself, and be patient.'

Then, turning to the constable, he continued his conversation with him aloud.

'What is your idea?'

'I think, sir, she has made up her mind not to return—in fact, to——'

'Ah! Why?'

'The room was in perfect order, and the child laid out——'

'The child?' exclaimed the Professor simply.

'Your daughter was not alone, sir,' said the inspector gently. 'She had a child——'

'Ah!'

'Which is dead.'

'Poor thing! She will die herself of sorrow. She was always so fond of little children, sir. They used to run to her whenever she appeared—which shows, sir, how loving her nature is, for children are keen judges of the heart. She will feel her child's loss very deeply.'

The inspector turned to the constable, and gave him directions to complete his search after the missing woman.

'Go to the river,' he added in a whisper. 'She had evidently but one idea in her mind when she left her lodgings. Perhaps you may be in time.'

As the man was leaving, the Professor begged that he and his friends might accompany him.

'You counsel patience, sir,' said he, 'but patience is impossible while we are here. The stillness of the place—the want of movement—renders our anxiety unbearable. You must, I am sure, see the reasonableness of my request. We shall do exactly as we are bid, sir, and, being all of us well acquainted with the child, our presence will add greatly to the probability of finding her.'

The inspector smiled lightly at the concluding argument advanced by the Professor, but yielded to his passionate pleading, all the more readily as he began to have a suspicion that the search would result in the finding, not of a living daughter, but of a corpse. As a precaution, however, against the display of any eccentric behaviour on the part of his visitors, he deputed the sergeant to take them under his personal charge.

A few moments later, the party left the station, the Professor—linked between his sister and Phillips—following close upon the constable and the sergeant. In this order they proceeded until they reached Westminster Bridge, when the two policemen came to a stop, and held a brief conversation together. At its conclusion, the constable went off in the direction of the river-side ; while the sergeant, beckoning to his charge to follow him, led the way to a sheltered position at the head of the bridge.

The wind was high, and swept in impulsive gusts round the corner of the adjacent building, stirring up from out-of-the-way places thick masses of dust and straw that had congregated together in fancied security, and whirling them with gleeful ardour into the eyes and down the throats of the unlucky passers-by. Heavy clouds, betokening rain, scudded swiftly across the sombre sky, so that when every now and then the mellow light of the full moon burst from its obscurity, it seemed as if an overhanging pall had been suddenly lifted away from the earth. It was a night when people who have homes hurry homewards, and congratulate

themselves upon having gained the welcome shelter
of its roof ere the storm that is brewing has burst
forth upon its mischievous course.

The Professor and his companions, huddled together to escape the wind and the dust, stood
eagerly watching the face of their impassive escort
in the vain hope of gathering from it a notion of
the thoughts that were passing through his mind.
An hour went by in this tedious manner, and then,
their patience having reached its limit, they were
about to protest against their inactivity, when a
low whistle was heard, which caused the sergeant
to relax his rigidity and become an ordinary flexible
mortal.

'Come!' he said.   'Follow me closely?'

The three poor creatures, half benumbed with
their long watch, had a difficulty in obeying him
as he led the way down a flight of stone steps on
to the Embankment.   At the bottom, the constable
joined them.

'She is close by,' he said, in a whisper. 'I have
followed her for half an hour along the Embankment.   She seems half crazy, muttering to herself
and singing childish songs.   She dropped this as
she went along.'

He held up a child's sock—a memento of the dead Angharad.

'Lead the way to her,' said the sergeant.

They went to a spot about a hundred yards off, and there, under a gas-lamp within a few paces of them, they saw the figure of a woman. She was leaning against the parapet of the Embankment, at a point where it was at its lowest height, looking intently upon the black river as it flowed beneath her. The sergeant held up his finger as a sign of caution; but the sight was too much for the pent-up feelings of the Professor, and he rushed forward, ejaculating in a quavering voice :

'Omega! My child !'

At the sound of his voice the woman started up and looked round for a moment upon her pursuers; then, with a wild cry of alarm, she threw herself into the fast-flowing stream.

The constable and Phillips rushed forward, but the sergeant, wiser than they, ran up the steps and made for the other side of the bridge, where a number of small boats were fastened to a wooden landing-place. Miss Hewitson remained by the side of her brother, supporting him with her arms, while he covered his eyes with his hands and wept as though his heart would break.

In a very few minutes the sergeant reappeared, bearing with him the dripping form of the woman. Though so short a time in the water, she had lost consciousness, and hung a lifeless mass over the shoulder of her rescuer.

'Look up, brother!' said Miss Hewitson. 'She is saved!'

The Professor rose from his anguish like a new man, and rushed to the sergeant.

'God bless you, sir!' he cried. 'God in heaven ever keep you under His sacred charge! Sir, I—I —cannot tell you all I feel towards you.'

The sergeant blushed—actually blushed—and hung his head, while the Professor put his arms round the drooping neck of his daughter, and kissed her cold cheek.

'Let us take her home at once,' he said. 'Poor creature, the cold has chilled her. Sir, you will let me take her home with me?'

The sergeant hesitated, for his duty forbade him to part with her; but, being human, yielded, and nodded his head in consent.

'Come, sister. Come, Phillips. Let us go at

once. Poor darling, she is cold and faint.' He leant over her, and apostrophized the lifeless form. 'My loved one ! it is I, your father, who speaks to you. Do you not know me ? It is your father, darling; speak, love, speak ! Oh ! my God, she is not dead ! Oh, spare me this sorrow ! No, no; it is only the cold that has chilled her—only the cold. How wicked of me to suspect that God would return her to my arms a corpse ! See, she breathes! O God, I thank Thee !'

In his thankfulness for this slight sign of life, he knelt down on the cold stones, and, lifting his hands to the black sky, opened his heart to the Almighty. His sister, fearful on his account, interrupted his thanksgiving, and raised him up gently.

'Come, brother. Your daughter needs rest and care. Let us go.'

They drove hurriedly away, bearing with them the still unconscious woman, and leaving the sergeant rooted to the spot on which he stood, with a sad feeling that his humanity had for once subordinated his duty.

CHAPTER IX.

THE sun rose gaily the next morning after a wild
night of storm and rain, and flashed its bright rays
against the windows of a small room on the second
floor of one of the modest tenements in Danes Inn.
Following their usual inquisitive bent, these giddy
little sun-rays made a desperate endeavour to force
their way into the room, but were met by an im-
perturbable Venetian blind, against which they ex-
pended their strength in vain.   At length, one more
enterprising than the rest found a narrow chink in
the enemy's armour, and, taking instant advantage
of its discovery, rushed frantically into the room.
This was the picture within.

An old man, pale and haggard from long unrest,
was bending over a low bedstead on which lay a
woman, whose features upturned wore the appearance of having already been touched by Death.   As
he peered down upon the motionless form, his hands

trembled with emotion, and his lips moved in prayer. In another part of the room, two women— an old and a young one—were standing side by side, looking with pitiful eyes upon the pathetic figure of the old man. It was a sad picture, and the sun-ray, whose nature was joyous, turned hastily and vanished through the chink into the fresh air again.

Towards noon, the sick woman, who had passed through the night in an unconscious state, raised her face from the pillow, and, opening her eyes, beheld the aged, drooping figure by her bedside. For a few moments she gazed with a look of incredulity, her eyes wandering over his person as though seeking for evidence of its reality; then, with a stifled cry, she sank back upon the pillow and buried her head in the bedclothes. The old man bent down still lower, until his face almost touched the straggling masses of black hair that alone were visible.

'Omega, darling!' he said, in a voice almost hushed to a whisper; 'it is I, your father. Look up, darling; let me see your dear face! I have been waiting for you so long; my heart was so empty without you. You cannot guess how great my joy is at having you back by me once more. I thank

God for sending you to me again.   I was so deso-
late without you; my life seemed to have lost its
flavour.   Darling, you hear me ? I am your father—
your father, darling ! Do you remember those happy
days when we used to take our walks together
about the hills and valleys of our dear Welsh home ?
How happy we were—how contented !   We were
in an earthly paradise.   Well, darling, we shall—
please God—enjoy again those delicious walks
among the old familiar scenes.   When you are
better, darling—and you will make haste to get up
from your sick-bed, will you not ?   To please your
father, whose happiness is inseparable from you.
Oh, if you knew how I have felt your absence;
how weary has been my life, how dead my heart!
Without my little Meggy I was like one that is
stricken blind.   The light of my eyes was gone; I
was left in sorrowing darkness.   Darling, you hear
me—your father ?'

The Professor paused, and waited in desperate
hope for a response; but none came, and with a
sigh, he rose from his stooping posture, and resumed
his melancholy watch.

At this moment the door opened, and admitted
Dr. Maddison.   He went to the bedside, and made

a silent examination of the poor creature, who lay with eyes shut and mouth stubbornly closed, feigning to be still unconscious. When he had finished, he crossed the room to Miss Hewitson.

'Can you not get him away?' he whispered. 'Try.'

Miss Hewitson, in obedience to his injunction, approached her brother.

'Brother,' she said, extending her hand to him, 'come away for a short while.'

'I cannot!' was the reply. 'I cannot exist away from her.'

Miss Hewitson slowly turned from him, and followed the doctor out of the room. Outside, they found Phillips.

'Well, what news?' he asked.

The doctor shook his head gravely.

'There is no hope,' he replied; 'she cannot recover. The shock upon her enfeebled constitution is too great. She may linger two or three days—no longer.'

Phillips looked at Miss Hewitson, and together they put another question.

'And he?'

'You must get him away—or there will be two deaths.'

Phillips cast a painful look at Miss Hewitson.

'We must save him,' he said; 'but how can we get him away?'

'Tell him what I have told you,' said the doctor. 'Tell him that there is no hope for his child.'

'Oh no!'

'There is no other way,' continued the doctor. 'Prepare him for the inevitable parting; it will lessen the blow when it falls, and you may prevail upon him to seek that rest which he is in so much need of.'

When the doctor had gone, Miss Hewitson and Phillips pondered over his suggestion.

'There is nothing else but to try it,' said Phillips at last. 'We must be cruel to be kind. We cannot afford to lose him.'

Together they entered the room; entering so softly that the Professor was unaware of their presence. He was bending over his daughter, making another appeal to her.

'My darling,' he was saying, 'it is not kind of you to keep this silence. I do not reproach you, dear, for I can imagine how scared your heart is by your troubles; but I am yearning so deeply for the sound of your dear voice. Speak to me, darling!

Are not your sorrows mine? We will share them together, and pray to God to send us peace. You are young yet, and I shall grow young again when I have you with me once more as of old. How happy we shall be, roaming among the well-remembered scenes of your childhood! Speak, darling! tell me that you hear me!'

Again there was no response, and again the old man sighed. Lifting his eyes, he saw his sister and Phillips watching him.

'I am so happy!' he said, with a faint smile. 'We shall never be parted again!'

Miss Hewitson glanced at Phillips, and Phillips at Miss Hewitson. Each read in the other's face that at that moment the task of undeceiving the Professor was too difficult to be performed.

It was not until the dusk was creeping into the room, and subduing human beings and inanimate objects into a common indistinctness, that the two conspirators found courage to carry out their project. In the all-pervading gloom, rendering it impossible to observe the expression on faces, they found it easy to approach the Professor and lead him between them to a distant corner. But here, while the Professor was wondering what was the matter, these poor, faint-hearted creatures fell a-trembling, and could not utter a word of what was on their minds.

'Well, sister?' at last observed the Professor.

'My dear brother,' she began, 'I—that is—Mr. Phillips——'

'Don't bring me in, ma'am,' said Phillips, in a fierce tone. 'Speak for yourself.'

'You have something to say, sister?'

'I have, brother, though I certainly expected that Mr. Phillips——'

'Why, in the name of goodness! Surely you——'

'I thought a man——'

'What! before a relative——'

'That makes it harder——'

'No, no——'

'I don't comprehend all this,' said the Professor, in a mild tone. 'What is it, Phillips?'

'Why do you ask me? Well, then, the fact is—Miss Hewitson, relieve me, for God's sake!'

There was a pause. Phillips shot a pleading look in the direction of Miss Hewitson; but, remembering that the darkness would deprive it of its effect, he put his hand out towards her, and whispered in a

tone sufficiently loud to be heard throughout the
room.

'Take it upon yourself.   Do!   I cannot speak!'

'Sister,' said the Professor, 'what do you wish to
say?   I am listening.'

Miss Hewitson, with an effort, called up all her
strength of character, and answered him in a firm
voice.

'Brother, we think you should leave your child
for a while and take a rest.   It is hard to tell you,
but it is better that you should know the truth.
Your work here is useless.   You cannot save her.
Forgive me, brother, for the pain I cause you.   But
it is with a good object.   She cannot recover; it is
hopeless to think of it.'

Another pause ensued, to be broken by Phillips.

'Dear old friend,' he said, putting his arm tenderly within the Professor's, 'we cannot help telling
you this.   It is—to keep you amongst us.   What
should we do without you?   You must take a rest.
Believe me, you cannot save your child.'

They could not see the effect of their words upon
the Professor, but, when he spoke, his voice though
subdued was perfectly calm.

I thank you both.   It is right that I should know

what you have told me. I cannot save her! Well
God's will be done! But I cannot leave her. I
must save her soul!'

'Think of yourself!' cried Phillips. 'Think of
your friends! For heaven's sake leave her for a
while—only for a while! My dear old friend—friend
of so many years—have pity on those who love you!
You need rest—take it; we will keep watch in your
absence. You need it so much. Do this, I pray—if
not for your own sake, for ours!'

'Have no fear for me,' answered the Professor,
laying his hand gently on that of Phillips. 'You
have ever been the best and dearest of friends to
me. I owe you a debt of gratitude for your firm
and steadfast friendship through so many trials that
I can never repay. But you would never bid me
neglect my duty. And it is my duty, as you must
see. She is nearing death, you tell me—well, I
must subdue my feelings in the one great work I,
her father, am bound to perform. She must not die
without imploring the forgiveness of the Almighty
for the sins which she has—unwittingly, I am sure
—committed against Him! You will feel, I know,
that I am right, after a little thought. Leave me,
then, dear, kind friends—leave me, I beg of you, to
my duty.'

They could urge no more, and, with swelling hearts, they retired, leaving the old man to continue his solitary watch by the bedside of his dying child.

During the livelong night he remained patiently by her side, making frequent appeals to her to abandon that attitude of determined silence which she still persisted in maintaining. But his words beat against a heart that had been hardened into stone by the buffetings of the world, and made no outward impression.

In the morning, when Dr. Maddison again visited the sick-room, he found his patient gradually passing away from life. The Professor was leaning against the wall at the top of the bedstead, with one hand placed on the back of an adjacent chair to support his weakened frame. With his pallid and careworn face, he looked the very picture of feebleness. In answer to the doctor's penetrating glance, he made an attempt to smile, murmuring in a low, broken voice :

'I am very happy here with her. We shall never be parted again.'

Outside the room, Dr. Maddison renewed his warning to Miss Hewitson and Phillips.

'He is visibly changed. If you don't get him away at once, his daughter's death will only be the forerunner of his own.'

In their distress, Miss Hewitson and Phillips determined to call in the aid of the Church, and a note was at once despatched to Harold, bidding him come without delay on an errand of life or death. In very quick time he arrived, and was made a repository of the deep feelings that stirred these poor creatures. In complete contrast to their ordinarily strong natures, they showed a weakness and hesitation that surprised Harold. They clung on each side of him, and poured their piteous tale into his ears; and, when they had done, stood and looked at him in anxious expectation that he would utter some brave words to comfort their stricken hearts.

Nor were they disappointed. With all the confidence of a young clergyman, who deems himself by right of his sacred office equal to the task of assuaging all human sorrows, Harold bade them lead him into the old man's presence.

'He says it is his duty to save his daughter's soul. Well, I may, without fear of his considering me an intruder, offer to assist, and, in assisting, I hope I may prevail upon him to entrust the task to me while he seeks the rest that is so necessary for him.'

He entered the room, and, merely glancing at Alpha, who was seated by the window silently nursing her grief, went to the old man's side. His voice was for a moment paralyzed at the sight of the wearied, haggard face before him, but, recovering himself quickly, he said :

'I have come to help you, sir, if you will allow me.'

'Thank you, you are very kind,' replied the Professor listlessly. 'She is too ill to pay much attention yet, but she will listen to me soon.'

Harold subsided into silence, his confidence in succeeding where Miss Hewitson and Phillips had failed being considerably damped by the old man's answer. He remained partly withdrawn from view, though this was unnecessary, as the Professor, fully occupied by his own thoughts, paid no further heed to him. Two or three hours passed thus—the Professor every now and again muttering a few soothing words into his mute child's ear, or making an endeavour to obtain possession of her hand beneath the bedclothes—when Harold bethought him of a new plan.

He came to where Alpha was sitting, and, taking her hand in his, led her to the bedside.

'Sir,' he said, 'we ask you, as two beings who have an absorbing interest in you, as two children of yours who look to you to be with them and guide them through many future years, to listen to our entreaty that you will take a short rest. You will not refuse us!'

'You are very kind,' was the calm reply, 'but I have no need of rest. I must not leave my child. The solemn duty that is imposed upon me will give me whatever strength I may require. My children, I bless you for your kind thoughts and loving care. Do not fear for me. I am sustained by hope. I thank you with all my heart.'

He turned away, and they, seeing that their task was hopeless, left him to continue his lonely watch.

The sunbeams danced and played without, tapping lightly against the blind, all heedless of the sorrowful gloom within, until the gathering pall of night cut short their brief existence. Still the old man bent over his dying child, hoping and hoping that his constant appeals would at last soften that obdurate heart, and entice into utterance the well-remembered voice.

Later on, when candles were brought in, Miss Hewitson, with the pertinacity of her sex, made a fresh attempt to overcome his obstinate refusal to seek rest; but it had no better success than all the former attempts.

'Do you not see,' he said, 'that what you ask is impossible ? My body might be away, but my heart would be here. How, then, could I find rest ?'

In his nervous state, the presence of others in the room—the bustling about and the whispering, for which Miss Hewitson was mainly accountable—became a species of torture, which developed to such an extent that, after looking round once or twice uneasily, he said :

'I should like to be alone with my child for a while. You will gratify me, I am sure.'

Miss Hewitson hesitated, but a word from Phillips, who was present, overcame her scruples, and she withdrew with the rest.

Left alone, the Professor bent down and made a desperate appeal to his daughter.

'Omega, darling, I conjure you by the love you

have for me to speak. My heart is breaking at your continued silence. They tell me you are dying—it is best that you should know—that you will soon be passing away from your earthly life to another. Which is that other life to be? Oh, my darling, by the memory of the happy days that we have passed together, I implore you to have pity on me, and speak. I would, my child, that God in His great mercy would take me to His bosom at the same moment, for what will life be to me when you are gone? If you knew how I love you! Oh, the weary past year! You cannot tell what I have suffered, bereft of you! We have met again, darling, but to be on earth together for a short space. Let us make our peace with God together, in the hope that He will unite us in the world to come! My darling, your father pleads to you—speak!'

He paused, and waited with beating heart for the sound of the voice he loved. It came not, but a quivering of her eyelids and a gentle movement of her hand from beneath the bedclothes seemed to betoken an awakening sensibility. The old man seized the hand and kissed it, and then, clutching it tightly between his own, knelt down by the side of the bed.

'My darling,' he said, in a hurried, joyful tone, 'let us ask God's pardon together for the sins we have committed against His name. The end is looming near; we have no time to spare. My heart is beating with hope! I know you will not deny me. It is but a short prayer, darling; the old one that in your childhood's days you used to repeat at my knee. You remember it well. Try to repeat it with me now.'

He raised his eyes above, and began in a low, solemn voice :

' " Our Father !" '

He waited, with a terrible tension at his heart, but her lips remained tightly closed. He repeated the words.

' " Our Father !" '

For fully five minutes he remained silent, straining his ears to catch even a whisper from her, but in vain. Overcoming a creeping sensation of bitter disappointment, he nerved himself once more to the task.

' " Our Father !" '

No sound broke from her, but, at the moment when despair was mastering him, he felt her fingers gently closing on his. With a sudden revival of hope, he uttered the words again.

' " Our Father !" '

Then, at length, his faith was rewarded, for the obstinate lips moved, and a low, whispering voice repeated his words.

' " Our Father !" '

Oh ! what a thrill of joy shot through his heart as he heard once again the tones of a voice that was more to him than the sweetest tones of the sweetest songstress that ever lived ! A low, harsh voice it was, but it fell upon the old man's ears like the music of the falling rain upon the ears of the thirsting traveller in the desert. Great tears of joy flowed from his eyes, and something rose in his throat, which for a short time prevented him from proceeding with the prayer. But the deep wish to wring from her an acknowledgment of her sins and a request for pardon made him put a quick check on his feelings. He continued, in a voice of enforced calmness :

' " Which art in heaven——" '

In a few seconds came the echoing words :

' " Which art in heaven——" '

' " Hallowed be Thy name——" '

A shorter pause ; then, in the same low whisper,

' " Hallowed be Thy name——" '

' " Thy kingdom come——" '

' " Thy kingdom come——" '

' " Thy will be done on earth as it is in heaven——" '

' " Thy will be done on earth as it is in heaven——" '

' " Give us this day our daily bread——" '

' " Give us this day our daily bread——" '

' " And forgive us our trespasses, as we forgive them that trespass against us——" '

The answering voice did not come at once, and the Professor, hearing the sound of a sob, looked down. He beheld a miracle—she was crying bitterly. It was some minutes before the prayer could be resumed, and then the Professor, with admirable patience and tact, led her on from sentence to sentence until the final ' Amen ' was reached. With this last word—the trumpet note of victory ringing in his ears—the old man buried his face in the coverlet, and poured forth his thanks to the One who had armed him for the fray.

The candles burnt lower and lower, and began to flicker and throw great shadows on the wall—still, he moved not. There was a portentous silence in the room, in the midst of which the tick-tick of the small clock on the mantelpiece sounded like the regular beat of a steam-hammer. This solemn stillness, which carried an indefinable dread with it, was at length broken by a tap at the door. It awoke no sound in return. A second tap followed, but with the like result. Then the handle turned, and Miss Hewitson entered, with Alpha and Phillips close behind her. She glanced at the bed. Her brother was still kneeling by its side with his face buried from view, clasping the hand of his child. She went softly up to him, and touched the two hands. A moment later she drew back in alarm.

'Brother!' she shrieked.

But there was no response. The old man and his child were both beyond the reach of human voice, for they were dead. The soul of the just man and the soul of the erring but repentant daughter had passed away at the same moment, to plead together before the judgment seat of the Almighty. Who that believes in God's mercy can doubt that on the great day to come they will both be admitted to share together the joys of eternity?

In the quiet churchyard of the parish in which

the little Welsh cottage so long tenanted by the Professor is situated, there are two unpretending graves lying side by side, in which repose the bodies of the old man and his daughter. Here, in summer-time, often come two couples—an elderly man and elderly woman and a young man and young woman, the latter accompanied by a little child. They bear with them wreaths of wild flowers, which they place reverently on the graves—small tokens of an undying respect and love. As they stand looking down on the green mounds, memory brings back to them the figure of the old man, whose life was great—not in the sense of brilliant victories achieved in war, or grand triumphs won in the Senate, but in the higher, truer sense of man's duty upon earth well and faithfully performed.

THE END.

REMINGTON AND CO., 134, NEW BOND STREET, LONDON.